TEN SHOTS QUICK

Stories of the New West

Trevor Holliday

Barnstork Press

ISBN-13: 9798797158561
ISBN-10: 1477123456

Cover design by: John Holliday
Library of Congress Control Number: 2018675309
Printed in the United States of America

To my many friends in Navajo County, Arizona.

CONTENTS

A REGULAR EVENING AT EDDIE C'S

"I heard Cavilee and them been coming into town a couple times."

Jim Phipps sat opposite Chance Downey with a look on his face, acting like he knew something.

What did Phipps know? Nothing.

Right now, neither Phipps nor Downey knew Cavilee's current situation.

Chance Downey nodded, not willing to look up from his cards. He had learned years ago how his particular facial expressions could betray his poker hand.

"I seen Cavilee up at the Circle K when I was getting gas the other day."

"So what?" Downey said. "It's a free country so far. Last time I checked it was."

Phipps's eyes went up to Downey's.

"Sure," Phipps said. "It's fine. Cavilee just looks like a tough hombre to me, that's all.

"Minding his own business?" Downey said. "He didn't scare you, did he?"

The other men laughed, except for Phipps, who looked back at his cards, finished with razzing Downey.

Billy Valentine didn't laugh either, but he wasn't a regular in the poker game and he sure as hell wasn't getting involved in whatever these two were talking about.

Billy Valentine was carefully not paying attention.

That was Billy Valentine for you.

"Why the hell would Charley Cavilee scare me? Doesn't he do some kinda work for you?" Phipps said. "I thought for sure he worked for you one time or another, making deliveries or some such. Something, anyway. Wasn't that Cavilee?"

Downey stared at his cards as if willing them to change into a better hand.

That was Downey.

Wishing for luck and looking downcast and bitter when it didn't come.

"Cavilee don't work for me," Downey said. "He's never worked for me."

Downey picked up a pack of Doral cigarettes from the table and pulled one out. Smoking low-tar now even though there was no taste to the things. Tapped the filter on the table where he had been nursing vodka and water.

He looked at Phipps, apparently not worried any more if he gave away his hand. His luck was sorry anyway, what the hell difference would it make?

A regular evening at Eddie C's.

Fluorescent lights flickered yellow in the back room of the steakhouse where the group of men played poker.

Phipps grinned at Downey. Phipps was having fun now. Sometimes it took all night to get a rise out of Downey, but he had accomplished it early tonight.

Phipps leaned back in his chair.

"Well, excuse the hell out of me then, Mister Downey. It was an honest mistake. I hope I haven't caused offense.

Downey growled. He lighted the cigarette and coughed.

Unique filter system or not, the smokes were killing him and he knew it.

Shook his head.

"Seems like you got plenty of time to speculate on these things, Jimmy."

"You two interested in playing another hand? My understanding was we were here to play poker," Henderson said.

Phipps smiled. Nodded.

Henderson the diplomat.

Billy Valentine had had enough.

He would sit this hand out. Never should

have sat down in the first place. The discussion between Phipps and Downey was of no concern to Valentine. He tossed his cards down on the green felt then felt his back decompress when he stood up from the table. He'd been sitting longer than he thought and a lot longer than he had intended. He would sit out the rest of the evening. Let the men get down to whatever business they had with each other.

No need to announce his intention.

"You giving up so soon, Valentine?" Downey said.

Valentine shrugged. Downey didn't care whether Valentine played one hand or twenty. His comment was designed to deflect attention from himself and it did.

"Too rich for you?" Henderson said. He laughed. Henderson liked laughing at his own jokes.

Valentine smiled.

"It's your skill level," he said. "I can't keep up with you gentlemen."

The men laughed. Valentine could play cards with anyone.

Valentine hadn't come here to play cards tonight. He had come to eat steak. He had a big day ahead of him and he wanted a good meal and then some rest before heading to Tucson.

He had been roped into playing a couple of hands of poker and had lost a trivial amount of money.

He had avoided getting sucked into the conversation between Downey and Phipps.

Big deal.

The game would get along fine without him. Valentine had done his bit. The steaks were good at Eddie C's and he came here to eat and for a change of scenery. Billy Valentine didn't come here to play poker.

This was not his favorite way to spend an evening.

Pastel caricatures of local men hung framed on the knotty pine walls behind the tables.

Some of the same men from the pictures sat around the table, studying the hands they were dealt like they were looking at hard math problems.

Valentine knew all of the men. Neither Chance Downey nor Jim Phipps was worth a shit. Henderson either, for that matter.

Not worth the powder to send them to hell. Valentine would usually humor the others at the table for a while. Then he would leave, go into the dining room, order a steak.

Valentine got up. Looked back at the card table. The men wouldn't notice his absence. Valentine didn't make any difference to them.

They would trade their money back and forth all evening just the same way they always did.

Valentine walked toward the swinging door separating the back room from the rest of Eddie

C's.

Theresa put him at a table near the kitchen and the cigarette machine.

She smiled at Valentine.

"Hey Billy," she said. "Had enough back there?"

Valentine grinned. Tossed the menu onto the table. Lighted a cigarette. Shook his head.

"You know that bunch," he said.

"I do know them, Billy."

"T-bone," he said. "Medium well, potato side. Salad bar."

The usual.

* * *

Valentine saw the other man come in.

Ronnie Dosela gave a quick hug to Theresa.

Some men cast a shadow wherever they go. Dosela was one of those men.

Dosela glanced at Valentine before sitting down.

Nodded.

Billy Valentine tapped the cigarette on the side of the glass tray.

Nodded back.

He barely knew Dosela, but he knew the man's reputation.

* * *

Ronnie Dosela went to the door of the back room and surveyed the card players at the table before turning back away. He was glad Billy Valentine was not playing poker with the men.

Dosela didn't want to involve Valentine who was sitting in the restaurant now. Both Dosela and Valentine were ignoring each other.

Dosela wore a fleece-lined Carhartt jacket over dark blue jeans and Roper boots. A black hat with a horse-hair band over his long braid of dark hair.

Dosela had left his Marlin, a .357 1894 short-barreled rifle holstered in the cab of his pickup. The gun was lever-action. East German Zeiss-Jena sights he bought from a German national in the parking lot of a beer garden outside the gates of Panzer Kaserne.

The Marlin would bring down an elk. Dosela knew he didn't need the rifle yet.

Dosela looked at the poker table. Gave it a real going over.

Chance Downey wasn't going to look at Dosela. Downey had seen him, but wasn't going to acknowledge Ronnie Dosela. Instead he turned beetle-brows toward his playing cards.

The other men in the back room of Eddie C's didn't notice Dosela. He went back into the dining room.

He had seen what he needed to see.

Theresa seated him across the room from Valentine.

She brought him a shot of whiskey with a beer chaser.

Dosela drank the whiskey.

Looked over at Valentine.

Neither man was interested in the other one's business.

"You getting something to eat?" Theresa stood next to him holding a menu.

Dosela looked up as if just remembering something.

He was in no hurry. He wasn't going anywhere.

"I'll take the chops you got," Dosela said.

Dosela waited.

The pork chops were edged in on the plate with green beans, mashed potatoes with gravy, and corn.

Dosela stayed until he was alone in the dining room.

Theresa brought him another beer.

"You here till closing, Ronnie?" she said.

Dosela looked up.

The place was shutting down. He didn't have to leave, not for a while, anyway. The kitchen staff would take a while cleaning up and Theresa wouldn't mind him being here.

He nodded at the beer.

"Just finish this one," he said.

"Take your time," Theresa said. "I got all night if you want."

The wait wasn't long.

The game was over in less than a half hour and the men came out, one by one from the back.

Chance Downey was the last to leave, smoking another cigarette and hitching up his pants before going out the door into the night.

* * *

The driveway to Downey's house, deep in the country club, was lined on either side with ponderosa pines. A snowplow wouldn't have much clearance going through to the front. The house was built in territorial style with a sloping roof and a wraparound porch. Dosela knew exactly how far the house was from the road. This time of year and at this time of night there wouldn't be anyone else on the road. In back of Downey's house a single strand barbed wire fence separated his property from reservation.

Two sets of laws and two different jurisdictions applied when you crossed the fence.

Dosela turned his truck around with the front facing the road. If he needed to get out quickly, he didn't need to waste time, nor did he care to leave paint from his truck on the bark of the trees.

* * *

Downey wasn't used to taking orders,

TREVOR HOLLIDAY

especially in his own house.

But here was Dosela, standing in front of Downey with the Marlin pointed directly at Downey's sternum.

Behind Dosela, the oak framed grandfather clock showed a couple of hours had passed since Dosela had spotted Chance Downey playing cards at Eddie C's.

His timing was good.

"Just pick up the telephone," Dosela said. "I'm not taking you through this again."

"These boys are tough," Downey said.

"So I understand," Dosela said. "Now pick up the phone."

The walls were knotty pine in the big room where Downey spent most of his time at home in an orange recliner next to a cast iron stove surrounded by igneous rock.

A family portrait of Downey and his wife, their sons and daughters, and their large extended family was wired up on the chimney.

The kids were grown now. Downey's wife spent most of her time in Mesa these days.

Downey had taken his glasses off and was rubbing the indentations on the sides of his nose. Stalling before picking up the phone.

He could have done without the evening of poker, you want to know the truth, but people talk and you want to know what they are saying, especially if it happens to be about you.

Seeing Dosela had rattled Downey. Now

10

Dosela had come into his house like he owned it.

"I'm picking it up, I'm picking it up," Downey said, but he didn't move toward the phone.

Dosela picked up the phone with one hand, still keeping the gun trained on Downey's chest.

"You pay these boys with cash or dope?"

Downey shook his head. Leaned toward the phone. Hesitated.

"Cash, Dosela. Not that it's any your business. I got nothing to do with dope."

"That's not what I heard," Dosela said.

"It's the truth."

It was not the truth and both men knew it.

"Cavilee's the boss, am I right?"

Downey nodded.

"He's the only one of them with any sense."

"Call them. Tell them you got something for them to do. I don't care what you tell them as long as they get to the place, the clearing outside Wonderland. They know the place."

Downey grumbled, but he picked up the phone and dialed a number.

"Tell them all to come," Dosela said. "Come one, come all. The more the merrier."

"You all need to be there," Downey said into the phone. "That's right, all of you."

Hunched over in the recliner, his hand gripped white on the receiver.

Dosela heard the man on the other end of the line.

"You sure?" Cavilee was saying. "I don't think

that's a good idea."

"Just bring 'em." Downey said. "Clearing near Wonderland."

Ronnie Dosela knew Charlie Cavilee. He'd gone to school with Cavilee, but he didn't know the others. Cavilee had always been in trouble. Dosela remembered his pockmarked face and greased ducktail. He was surprised Cavilee was not in prison.

Downey got up.

"Sit back down, Chance," Dosela said.

Dosela's gun was still level with Downey's chest.

"Back in the chair, Downey," Dosela said. "Keep sitting in that chair."

"We can talk," Downey said. "You're making a mistake."

Dosela shook his head.

"No mistake," he said. "You need to sit down. I won't tell you again. You get up and you force me to make a mess. Nobody wants to clean up after that."

Downey sat back in the chair. His nose itched, but he didn't touch it.

Three shots met Downey. Quick shots one after another.

Dosela's shots hit the center of Downey's chest.

The pattern no bigger than a deck of cards.

✻ ✻ ✻

The keys to Downey's Cadillac were on the kitchen counter where Downey had left them coming back from Eddie C's.

Easy to find, right there next to a pill caddy and an oversized wooden spoon and fork hanging on the wall.

Dosela thought about taking the Cadillac out into the woods and then thought the hell with it. You don't want to get too cute with something like this. Somebody was going to find Downey, and eventually somebody was going to find Cavilee and his crew. There was no reason to tie the deaths together. Let the investigator's put their thinking caps on.

He'd do it the way he planned.

He looked back at Downey's body slumped on the recliner. Downey got off easy. The bullets would have stopped his heart immediately and he'd only had a few moments when he had probably been sure he was going to die.

Killing Cavilee and the others would be pointless without killing Downey. You chop a rattlesnake in half, the head can still kill you.

Downey was the snake and he had plenty of venom.

If Dosela had let him live Downey could always have found himself another Cavilee.

Dosela hadn't touched anything in the house. He turned away from Downey's body and left, wiping the front door before stepping off the front porch. The lights were on in Downey's house. He figured they would be on all night. It didn't matter. Downey lived deep in the woods, far enough from the road nobody would notice them blazing.

Somebody would find the body soon enough.

Dosela turned the key in his truck and drove his pickup through the winding country club streets, back to the main street of the town. The street was empty. He turned left, toward the reservation and drove, occasionally looking in the rear view mirror.

His plan was to drop his truck at home. It would take less than an hour to walk to Wonderland. He would be there waiting for Cavilee and the others.

* * *

Dark clouds above the ponderosa pine trees passed over the nearly full moon.

The three men sitting in the cab of the Ford pickup would be dead within minutes, but they didn't have an inkling about that. And because they didn't know these were their last few moments on earth, they were spending their time bickering over nothing.

They had been talking about old school Phoenix Suns basketball and then they had moved on to a discussion about rodeo.

Nothing gave them a hunch about what was

going to happen. They had worked for Downey before. Cavilee was the go-between, and Yazzie and Walker had been surprised the big man wanted to see them too, but Cavilee said it was probably a good thing and they should keep their mouths shut.

One of them though, Clyde Yazzie, was pissed. Yazzie was upset because he not only had to use his own damn car, but also because he had to fill the Duster with gas. With rising prices, fill-ups were expensive.

Yazzie had parked the Duster next to the truck in which the men were seated. Just a couple of years old, but the Plymouth was showing wear from hard use on the reservation's cinder roads.

"Plus," Yazzie said, "the son-of-a-gun's a gas guzzler. It'll deliver you the speed, but somebody's gotta pay for that kinda performance and so far that somebody is me."

"You're getting the money later," Cavilee said. "We gone over this. The man's paying us. Keep your damn gas receipts."

"I ain't keeping no doggone receipts," Yazzie said. "This isn't some regular thing. Plus, then I got evidence on me."

"That's the dumbest thing you said in the last few minutes," Cavilee said. "Maybe dumbest in a while. You just buy gas, all right? All you got to do is save the damn tape and the man will reimburse you. All you got to do is walk your ass into the Circle K and get the damn receipt."

Yazzie wasn't buying it.

"You telling me you never looked on one of them receipts? They got your time, place, date all on that thing. You might as well give them your damn social security number. They can track you down with one of them things, bro."

"You talking about the law? They look that close, they already found you, bro."

Cavilee was tired of the conversation. Tired of Yazzie's company.

"Go ahead and pay for the gas yourself. I don't give a damn one way or the other."

"Duster uses a lot of gas," Yazzie said. "That's all I'm saying. I'm just saying that."

Chadley Walker was quiet. Just like he was always quiet. He'd taken a baggie of dope from his pocket. Down to seeds and stems, the shit barely covered the bottom of the zip-lock. He rolled a joint and then licked the gummed edge of the Zig-Zag paper. He scooched forward in the cab and pulled a wooden kitchen match from the front pocket of his blue jeans. Like the jeans, the match was grimy. Walker scratched the tip of the match with the long thumbnail of his right hand and the sulfur head exploded, momentarily illuminating the truck cab and the faces of the three men.

"Three on a match's bad luck, Chadley," Yazzie said.

Walker nodded his head up and down. He knew the superstition. He cupped the match with his hand and lighted the joint and quickly shook the match.

"That's also a stupid thing to say," Cavilee said. "Maybe if there were three joints or something. Not three of us. That ain't bad luck at all. What you just said was stupid as hell."

"Don't make no difference, man," Yazzie said. "Some things you don't wanna mess with."

Walker, holding the smoke deep in his lungs nodded his assent.

He exhaled and passed the lighted joint to Yazzie.

Yazzie took the joint from Walker and looked over at Cavilee who slouched behind the wheel of the truck.

"When's the dude supposed to show up, bro? Seems like we been waiting for a while."

They had been parked about seven minutes.

* * *

The men couldn't see outside the cab. They only saw their own reflected faces in the windshield of the truck. They couldn't see Yazzie's Duster parked near them, and they couldn't see into the stand of ponderosa which surrounded the clearing.

They were parked at the end of a road maintained for use by logging vehicles. This time of year there would be no traffic here. They were by themselves.

In the woods, Ronnie Dosela watched the

truck.

He wore a black t-shirt and a jean jacket and he had smudged his eyes. He watched the men. They weren't going anywhere. He lightly applied pressure to the trigger of the Marlin. There was no rush. This was easy.

The three men were waiting for Chance Downey to show up.

Dosela knew who they were waiting for, and he knew Downey wouldn't show up.

Chance Downey had followed directions with Dosela in front of him, pointing the Marlin at him.

Downey did a good job under pressure.

Dosela had described the drop spot and told Cavilee how to get there. Downey told Cavilee to bring Yazzie and Walker too.

Cavilee brought them.

❋ ❋ ❋

Walker took a long drag on the joint. The red tip burned brightly.

He handed it to Yazzie who inhaled.

Dosela watched the spark illuminate the night.

Cavilee held the joint which Yazzie passed to him.

Three on a match was bad luck.
Not this. This was different.

* * *

Dosela sighted the three men. They were nested like fledglings in the truck.

The first shot entered the center of Cavilee's forehead.

The other two men's reactions were slow from the dope, but they were also trapped inside the truck.

The second shot killed Yazzie.

Walker, still unaware of what was really happening, died last.

THE COLD HARD FACTS OF LIFE

Nobody writes songs about heading back east on Route 66.

The songs you hear on the radio only deal with heading west. Nobody wants to talk about the trip going back.

Kent Pernell was almost home.

The windshield, grill, and hood of Kent's 1976 Grand Prix were splattered with bugs from a morning of driving into the rising sun.

You get those when you drive on Route 66 in the summer. Big bodied grasshoppers made a mess out of the Grand Prix's custom sparkle paint job. The insects had come down out of the sky like an Old Testament plague.

Then there is the heat which can bring a man to his knees. Waves of heat radiating from the road.

Mirages.

There was something wrong with the Grand

Prix. The car had been sputtering for two miles and Kent knew he needed to pull over in the rest stop ahead. Stepping out of the Grand Prix at the rest area, Kent smelled rubber. The kind of rubber you get with a hot radiator. He popped the hood and did a quick inspection. Unh-uh. Kent wasn't about to put his hand on the cap and risk losing whatever fluid was in there.

He wasn't carrying water, which was a big mistake in the desert. There was a lot of engine in the Grand Prix and he'd seen what over-heating could do.

Kent had already spent too much customizing the car for Ginny's taste. She'd give him holy heck if the engine blew.

He looked around the rest area. No water spigots to be seen.

Kent Pernell had not had a successful western trip. Nobody was buying. But he made good time on the way back. He always did. He stood mopping his brow with the last white perma-prest handkerchief Ginny packed for him before the trip. Two per day.

When it cooled down from the angry heat, Kent would use one of the hankies to open the radiator cap.

There were no other car parked, but two men stood in the back part of the rest area under a ramada.

You see all kinds of people on the road.

Kent knew Route 66 about as well as

anybody. Better than most of the people he saw heading west on the cracked asphalt two lane toward the Golden State. Kent passed many of them.

Families looking for something better than what they left behind. Chasing a dream they'd seen on TV.

There were lots of songs about the Golden State.

But nobody wrote songs about return trips.

These men at the rest area were different.

These men were probably hitchhikers.

Kent saw them as soon as he got out of the Grand Prix at the rest area.

A pair of men. At a glance, Kent couldn't tell their age. The men needed haircuts and shaves. Dirty from road grime, sweat, and sun.

Despite the heat, they had a little campfire going between the two of them.

Kent just needed to take a leak and stretch his legs. He'd been driving hard since Barstow.

He had already gotten a bad case of the creeps listening to Porter Wagoner singing *The Cold Hard Facts of Life* on the radio.

That's the one where the man decides to go home early and a stranger is there with his wife. The song had always given Kent the chills from the first time he heard it, but he listened anyway.

The man was telling his story from prison. He wonders if he will rot in prison before he goes to hell.

Kent hated being away from home.

He had to step wide around the men to get to the porta-potty.

Kent held one of the handkerchiefs over his nose, pulled the fresh cotton out of the roll dispenser, nudged the door back open with the toe of his black penny loafer. The place might as well have been a hobo jungle with the two men hanging around. Kent's father talked about these places from back during depression days.

Kent's dad called men like these two *down-and-outers. Hooverville residents.*

His dad told Kent stories about growing up before the war. Back in the Dirty Thirties.

Men came into Holbrook riding the rails, landing down by the Bucket of Blood.

"Those were bad times," his dad said. "They weren't always bad men. Some were just down on their luck. It was hard times."

Kent hadn't been born yet. He was born two years before Pearl Harbor.

One of the bums at this rest stop was tall and the other one was short. The two of them were like Mutt and Jeff in the funny papers.

"Hey Mister," the taller one said, "Hey Mister Traveling Man.

Kent ignored the man.

Smoking a rolled up cigarette, the taller one kept looking at him. The other man was cooking Van Camp pork and beans over a fire made from scrap plywood. The greasy black smoke smelled foul.

Where the hell had these two been the last thirty years?

A man could get a job today.

Kent figured maybe the man wanted to clean his windshield, run a dirty rag over the green paint of the Grand Prix. Like hell. Kent wouldn't let either one of these fellows near his Grand Prix. Maybe if they had some water, but even then probably not.

"Hey Mister Traveling Man," the man said again. "I need to talk to you for one minute at the absolute, very most."

The man grinned. A rack of shiny white teeth emerged from a long face under slicked hair.

Long white teeth like the ivory keys on a piano.

Kent walked toward the man.

Kent's family had survived the depression. Kent's dad had a hardware store. He had kept the place going, but it nearly killed him.

"I just need to talk to you a second," the man said. He was holding something in his left hand. That something looked like paper folding money, like he had a real bankroll held together in a silver clip.

Like hell it was a real bankroll.

Kent knew this character wouldn't have two wooden nickels to rub together let alone a roll of bills. This was some sort of a con game the guy meant to run.

If they had just rolled some rube down the road somewhere, Kent didn't want to know about it. The tall man held the money out and joggled his hand slightly, like the motion you make to get a dog to come up next to you.

Kent hitched up his Ban-Lon trousers. He'd lost weight and now he used the next-to-last notch on his belt to hitch up the stretchy fabric.

"What you got, buddy?" Kent said. He grinned. "Looks like you just knocked off the First National Bank."

Kent laughed at his own joke, but the tall man with the white teeth only slightly grinned. The small man sitting next to the fire shook his head and pushed a rectangular piece of the plywood into the fire with the toe of his busted out brogan. The small man didn't smile at all. He extended the bent fingers of his dirty hand toward the taller man.

Snapped two of those fingers like a king summoning a knight to join him around the round table.

The tall man peeled a bill from the roll and handed it to the man by the fire. He winked at Kent and looked like he would have nudged him in the ribs if Kent was closer.

"Betcha never seen nothing like this, old buddy," the tall man said.

He handed one of the bills to the man by the fire.

Kent looked more closely. This was a real nofooling five dollar bill. Enough money to buy these two men hamburgers and smokes.

The smaller man held the bill up so Kent could see it. It looked brand new. No grime on the five-spot like you see on a bill passed hand to hand to hand.

The small man held the fiver between his index and middle finger. He wore a big ring with a red stone under the large joint of his middle finger. It looked like a class ring.

Maybe from the same source as the money clip.

Kent watched the smaller man hold the bill next to the plywood fire. He held the fiver about as close as a moth will go to a candle flame.

The bill eventually caught fire.

The man held on as long as possible while the fiver turned to ash, then dropped the bill into the blaze.

"Looks like you two got money to burn," Kent said.

He laughed, then waited for the men to laugh.

They didn't. Instead, the taller one motioned for Kent to sit by the fire.

It wasn't much of a fire. Just a couple pieces of scrap plywood, some painted, and the can of beans. They coulda bought more than a can of beans with their money, but since they didn't ask, Kent figured he would mind his own beeswax.

Kent didn't want to get his trousers dirty.

The little man was sitting on a crate and there wasn't anything else to sit on other than bare ground.

Kent hitched his trousers up again and went down into a squat.

He looked over his shoulders. There were no cars other than his in the rest area. He opened his hands.

"All right, fellows," he said. "I'm listening. What's your game?"

"Ain't no game, stranger," the man by the fire said. "Jerry called you over here for a purpose. Now what do you suppose this purpose was he had in mind?"

Jerry grinned. White teeth showing below slick hair.

Kent shrugged.

"Search me," he said. "You two came into a fortune, and you want to share it with me. You have charitable instincts."

Jerry laughed. A high pitched cackle.

"You might as well tell him about it, Philly. Time's wasting."

Philly motioned to Jerry again. An impatient gesture. Jerry handed him the roll of bills.

"You know about icebergs?" Philly said.

"Not intimately," Kent said.

"Let me give you a little education, then," Philly said. "Them things float around the ocean, right? You see one, your ship's gotta stay away on account of they got more ice under the surface of the water than they got ice up top. You with me so far?"

Kent stood up.

First of all, the squatting posture was uncomfortable.

Secondly, he was afraid the strain might burst the stitching, and he needed these trousers to last.

Finally, he didn't need a lecture on icebergs.

"Get to the point," he said.

Icebergs.

Jerry shook his head.

"He's getting to it," he said. Jerry sounded menacing.

Kent should have stayed away from these men.

"All right," Philly said. "Point is, there's more damn ice under the surface than there is on top."

"That's right," Jerry said. He nodded vigorously. "Man's telling the truth."

"What's all this got to do with the price of tea in China?" Kent said.

Philly laughed. His laugh was different from Jerry's. Philly's laugh was low. Phlegm rattled in a wheeze from his lungs. He held up the roll of bills and waved it at Kent.

"The point?" he said. "The damn point is there's more of these where they come from. More than enough to make a man very wealthy. If not for the rest of his days, at least for a while. There's money beyond your imagination. Whatever you make in your job, stranger? Double it. Triple it. Put a zero or two on the end of it and multiply. That's how much money we can get. And it's all there for the taking."

"Like fun," Kent said. "You two would present a different figure if you had that much money, unless you just love living out here on the road."

"Hear that, Jerry?" Philly looked up at the taller man who was shaking his head. "Another non-believer."

He turned back to Kent.

Pointed at the Grand Prix.

"Go ahead on then," he said. "Nothing more for you to see or hear from us. Get back in your fancy car and sell your wares."

"Parts," Kent said. "I sell car parts."

Philly fanned the roll of money in his fingers. There were tens and twenties in the roll besides the five he'd burned.

Kent remembered his father telling him that in the carnival world and elsewhere, the largest bill often is placed on the outside to make the roll look more impressive.

Philly's roll was made up of big bills all the way through.

Kent squatted down again.

"All right, Philly," he said. "You got my attention, now. I'm listening."

Philly looked at Jerry.

"Hear that, Jerry? The man's listening. Don't

wonders never cease? And it seems we're on a first name basis. I guess money does talk."

Jerry's grin now extended across his face. More of the white teeth were exposed.

"You won't be sorry, stranger," Jerry said. "A man only meets opportunity every once in a while. It ain't an everyday occurrence."

A stench came from the mouth of Jerry. If the man had brushed his teeth twice in the last year, Kent would have been surprised. He remembered reading in a movie magazines that Clark Gable himself suffered with halitosis coming from bad fitting dentures. This could be the same situation with Jerry and his very white teeth. However, dentures weren't cheap, and these two, despite the money clip, looked like they had been out on the road for some time.

The bills looked legitimate, but Kent knew you had to be wary of counterfeit money. Another caution from his father.

"You go to the fair and get change?" Kent's father said, "You get change, you might as well put a sign up saying 'hello, I want to be robbed today.'"

"This money is all right?" Kent said.

Philly shook his head no and gave Kent a pitying look.

"Take a look yourself, you think that," Philly said. He tossed the roll of bills to Kent as casually as if he was throwing over a rolled up sports section.

"Take a look," Philly said. "Look all you want. It's as real as the hairs on your head."

Kent involuntarily put his hand to his head. He felt a chill.

* * *

"Don't come any closer," Philly said. "I gotta be able to see you."

Kent stopped.

"I wasn't planning to come any closer than this. Matter of fact, I'm just going to head back to my automobile and drive on down the highway. So, I'll be saying *adios amigos*."

The Grand Prix was steps away, unlocked. Kent hoped like hell the thing had cooled down, but he doubted it.

Even if the car seized up on him, he'd be away from these two.

Philly poked the fire again with the toe of his shoe.

"Hear that, Jerry? Sounds like he speaks Mexican, too."

Jerry showed his teeth again. Turned to Kent.

"You got any tailor-made cigarettes, Traveling Man?"

Kent laughed.

"Bankroll like you fellers have, you two smoking roll-your-owns?" Kent tapped his shirt pocket. Pulled out a pack of Lucky Strikes took one for himself and shook two more out for Philly and

Jerry. He fanned the roll of bills. Just as he'd seen. Tens, twenties. Some ones and fives, but not many. They didn't look new, nor were they beat to hell.

Philly pulled a branch from the fire and lit the cigarette with the glowing ember at the top. Waved the stick up and Jerry also lighted his cigarette.

Kent flipped the top from his lighter and wheeled up a flame.

"So, you play cards?" Philly said.

"You asking me if I want to play?" Kent said. "I'll be on my way now. I'm not interested in cards."

"Traveling Man," Jerry said, "Philly don't want to play cards with you. He's just asking, do you play cards."

Kent played poker only occasionally.

"I'm no expert, but I've played."

Philly nodded.

"You're honest, then, I can tell. What would you say if I told you a way you could make a bundle of money, bigger than the one you're holding in your hands. Guaranteed."

Philly motioned for the roll of bills. Kent felt a tug of regret, throwing it back toward the man by the fire.

Kent thought about the situation waiting for him at home. His job was not stable, and the trip had not been successful. This could be his last sales trip, depending on the boss.

He had never done well in that part of California. He was not well liked in Barstow. There was something about the accounts there. They didn't like him and never would.

They liked his predecessor.

Arnie. Everybody liked Arnie Malden. Everybody liked Arnie Malden better than they liked Kent Pernell.

Kent was sweating now. For the first time, he was thinking about the money Philly held in his fingers. Money which would solve Kent's problems.

The song kept going through his head.

The damn Porter Wagoner song.

Who taught who the cold hard facts of life?

These hobos were playing him for a fool.

Kent knew he should leave. Just walk back over to the Grand Prix, do something about the radiator, get back on the road.

There had to be water in this rest area. Kent just hadn't seen any yet.

By dinner time, he would be pulling back into the little house on Florida Street where Ginny would have dinner ready for him.

Kent's father's words had been clear.

Don't trust a man who has made his life on the road.

These old boys probably hadn't started out like this. Nobody does. The grime on their skin alone took time.

Kent stopped.

Ginny.

How much dough had there been in just that roll he'd thrown back to Philly?

Two hundred? Three hundred? The amount had to be greater than that.

Virginia deserved a better life, didn't she.

Better than the life he'd been able to provide with the parts route.

He was going nowhere in his career. It was time to face it.

"What was that about cards?" he said.

"We'll skip that part," Jerry said. The tall man pulled a toothpick from his front pocket. He poked it through the nub end of the Lucky Strike and held the last of the smoke in front of him. Still crimson and gray at the end.

Jerry inhaled.

"We need your car," he said.

Kent stared at the men then looked at the Grand Prix.

"It's not my car," he said. "It belongs to my boss."

Why was he telling these men anything? They didn't need to know about the car.

"We need it." Jerry stepped closer.

A blade in Jerry's hand flashed.

"This is close-up magic," Jerry said. "I got the knife, you got the car.

Kent stepped back but Jerry had him by the collar and held the knife to his neck.

From this distance Kent could smell the tall man's foul breath.

"Move slow while you give me the key, Traveling Man," Jerry said.

Kent felt the tip of the blade on his neck.

The two men got in the Grand Prix and drove away, Jerry driving.

Kent watched. He took his handkerchief from his pocket and held it to his neck.

Philly and Jerry wouldn't get too far, though.

Not with that radiator.

There were no other cars in the rest area. No pay phones.

Kent looked at the ashes in the fire. A couple of charred ends remained of the bills.

They had been bogus, just as he originally suspected.

One was stamped *for stage-use only*.

Kent had been taken and he knew it.

He'd learned something about the cold hard facts of life.

His father had been right. You see all kinds of people on the road. There wasn't anybody here in the rest area yet. Still, he might be able to get a ride from here, even though the sun was going down.

THE PROPER RITUAL

"Come up tomorrow, Mister Waterman," Irma Dosela said. "Find out about our people. Treat us like your family. Treat us like we are your own people."

Randall Waterman shook his head. He took the phone slowly away from his ear and looked out the plate glass window of the bank building in Tucson. The sky was pitch black from the eighth floor.

There was no view of the mountains at this hour.

They were there, of course. You just couldn't see them in the dark.

The only things visible now were well below Waterman, bathed in the orange street lights of downtown Tucson. In the distance, the neon sign for the Congress Hotel and the black entrance to the Fourth Avenue underpass.

Irma Dosela was calling late tonight. He shouldn't have picked up the phone. If she had come from a tribal meeting, she would be wearing her fancy traditional dress of pleated satin and her squash blossom necklace. If she was home she was probably in the jeans and sweatshirt she'd worn the first time he'd met her when he'd driven out to her house just outside town. She had been mixing dough in a steel bowl and had greeted Waterman happily.

Tonight, Irma Dosela was two hundred miles of winding roads and steep canyons away from Waterman.

Randall Waterman was used to her calls. Irma Dosela held an important position on the Tribal Council. She had a chair two seats down from the chairman where she took notes. Waterman couldn't afford to get on her bad side.

This was late for her to call. How would she have known Waterman stayed at the office this late?

Your own people.

Who were Waterman's people, anyway?

Randall Waterman looked out the plate glass window and down. Three men stood by one of the street lights. This late and on this particular corner they were most likely conducting a dope deal.

Waterman watched them pass a brown paper bag hand to hand.

Winos, not druggies.

A police car passed slowly and the men moved closer to the sheltering building.

People *did* look like ants from this height.

Waterman fingered the Windsor knot on his paisley Countess Mara tie. He thought about Irma Dosela's reference to his own people.

What did she know about his family? Her ideas of Waterman's family were probably based on television. Like Waterman was one of Fred MacMurray's three sons.

Fair enough. Waterman's ideas of Native culture were also based on television.

Family.

These Indians didn't want Randall Waterman giving them the *Waterman* family treatment.

Randall Waterman was not happy thinking about his own family. He had spent a long time distancing himself from his family and their endless backyard barbecues. Thinking about the men in his family with their beer guts and the women with their beehive hairdos only brought Waterman down.

Irma Dosela didn't want Waterman treating her people the same way he treated his own family. Waterman avoided his own family.

At least his father's family provided Waterman with a claim to Native American ancestry.

Cherokee on his father's side was the story.

After digging around, Waterman confirmed that his great-great-grandmother had been born in the Indian Territory long before Waterman's father's parents came to Arizona.

The grandmother hadn't been Cherokee though, she was Pawnee.

This relationship was not enough for Waterman to claim tribal status, but it was something upon which to hang his hat when he met Irma Dosela.

Oh yes, my people are Pawnee.

It took practice, but Waterman could now say it smoothly.

Waterman brought the phone back closer to his ear. Perched it between his chin and neck.

Irma Dosela was still going on and on. Waterman found it difficult to follow what she was saying.

Something about Pete Silver.

Waterman had met Silver at the last tribal meeting. Probably a medicine man, but nobody said so in so many words. Nobody was going to tell Waterman anything like that.

Silver's hair had been pulled back in a ponytail, he wore a faded denim jacket, and he had a face which, when younger, could have taken him to Hollywood.

Silver gave a rambling invocation at the start of the meeting. He'd cleared his throat and started in, speaking mostly in Apache, but with just enough English to make Waterman sit up and pay attention. Words like 'big bucks' and 'target area' made Waterman uncomfortable.

It was possible Pete Silver's monologue had

nothing to do with Waterman.

Anything was possible.

Pete Silver had voiced concern about the placement of the proposed casino and had tried to catch up with Waterman at the end of the meeting. Waterman had managed to dodge Silver.

Silver didn't worry Waterman, but Ronnie Dosela did.

Waterman had seen Irma Dosela's nephew.

Ronnie Dosela looked tough and he also looked unhappy with Waterman.

It would be best to get along with Irma Dosela.

Irma Dosela had pointed her nephew out to Waterman. The younger man sat cross legged on one of the folding chairs in the back row. Staring straight ahead. Green bandanna and dark glasses. Betraying no emotion.

Waterman looked down at the Tucson street lights from the window again.

A police car cruised down the street. The three men had disappeared.

The street was empty from the Chicago Music Store to the Wig-o-Rama.

Irma Dosela had stopped talking on the phone. She was waiting for a response from Waterman.

"Of course, Mrs. Dosela," Waterman said. "Whatever would give you the idea I'd treat your people in any other way?"

"I just want to tell you this ahead of time, Mr.

Waterman."

She had made this point during each of the previous conversations.

"Of course, Mrs. Dosela."

Nodding vigorously as if the woman was standing in front of him.

"Hey," she said. "It's late. I gotta go. I gotta *skedaddle*."

That was the actual word she used.

It made Waterman smile.

Skedaddle.

What kind of word was that, anyway? She probably learned it from a western movie thirty years ago.

Sheriff, I swear, them boys just up and skedaddled.

Waterman heard a dial tone. Irma Dosela always ended her calls abruptly.

He placed the phone back on the receiver.

Carefully.

Never a slam.

Waterman had learned a little bit about controlling his emotions at a seminar held last year at the Ramada Inn on Miracle Mile.

Disassociate.

Detach.

Depart.

The seminar leader wrote those three words on the white-board in front of the room then circled them and drew arrows pointing toward them.

41

TREVOR HOLLIDAY

Randall Waterman felt himself walking away from the plate glass and sitting down in the micro-fiber recliner next to his desk.

Disassociating.

Felt himself closing his eyes.

Detaching.

The technique usually worked. He had paid two hundred and seventy five dollars and had given up a full weekend to learn the technique in the crowded Ramada Inn seminar .

Waterman encountered problems at the seminar.

The first problem was being told to sit in a circle during the seminar and not being allowed to freely go to the restroom. The leader, wearing black framed glasses, a black turtleneck, and chin-length mutton chop sideburns, made that clear.

Much of the conference was a blur, but Waterman had met a woman who eventually turned out to be a disaster.

After the seminar was over, the woman called him and left messages for weeks. He found out later she had continued to the next level of training and had been assigned the task of calling Waterman.

Asking him if he wanted to attend follow-up training.

Despite the problems, the meditative technique Waterman learned at the seminar worked to some extent.

Waterman sank into the recliner. Exhaling

deeply and concentrating on the outer level of his dermis, Waterman willed himself away from the office, watching himself drifting away from the plate glass window, the green carpets, the framed golf prints.

Departing.

Waterman pictured himself on the beach, watching the sun dropping down over the horizon, leaving orange and purple streaks in the sky. Randall Waterman concentrated. Felt the white sand beneath his feet and felt the gentle sea breeze landing on his face just right. Air conditioning, but effective.

Bring yourself into a relaxed, meditative state.

Then he heard the voice again. Pete Silver.

This was the old man who Irma Dosela insisted Waterman meet.

Repeating those words. Not words, really. A series of moans Pete Silver had repeated while looking into the small flame from the mesquite fire.

Pete Silver had been amused by Waterman's name. He had gotten a big laugh out of it.

"Waterman," he said. "That's a good one. We can *use* more water up here, Waterman. You stick around here you will be more than welcome."

Hilarious.

Waterman kept his mouth shut. He had smiled and nodded his head when Pete Silver performed the ceremony.

What the hell? Waterman could put up with

a little hocus pocus. What did he care so long as he got the papers signed?

Then Silver closed his eyes. Sank into what was maybe supposed to be a trance, but looked no different from sleep.

Waterman's eyes snapped open. This old man. This old *medicine man.*

Pete Silver stood between Randall Waterman and the deal and was the real reason for Irma Dosela's call.

Pete Silver needed to see him one more time Irma Dosela told Waterman.

Of course, he couldn't call Waterman himself.

They would meet tomorrow in the parking lot of Bashas' Supermarket.

What was the issue, anyway? You buy land. Buying land should be no more difficult than buying bread and milk at the corner store. People have sold land since the dawn of time.

Since antiquity, right?

So what was the difference with making a deal for this land? Not very damn much.

Waterman wasn't buying the land anyway. He was simply putting together a deal where tribal lands could be used for a casino. A casino which would bring money to the tribe.

Waterman wasn't offering beads and trinkets here.

This was cash.

And the promise of more to come.

The tribe would own the land, own the casino, provide the workers.

Waterman would provide management and guidance in his consultant's role.

In the past few months, Waterman had sat through endless tribal meetings.

Long? Tedious? You don't know the half of it, cowboy.

Native Americans did things different.

Who didn't know that?

Cue the soundtrack:

How the West Was Won.

So what?

Everybody wants money.

Waterman wanted money.

The tribe wanted money.

The people who would go in and pull quarters out of their white plastic cups to drop in the slots?

Guess what?

They were going to want money too.

Money makes the world go round.

Everything would work out like a happy little dream.

The deal was set. No matter what anybody said, the paperwork would be signed this weekend.

No matter what *anybody* said.

But then Pete Silver, with his greasy coat and ponytail, came in and got Irma Dosela's attention.

If Pete Silver needed to meet with Waterman before he would sign the agreement, Waterman would meet with him.

Pete Silver would do some Indian things. Silver had brought a pouch of cornmeal and an eagle feather to the council meeting Waterman attended. Silver performed some kind of ceremony and Waterman smiled respectfully.

No doubt the next meeting would be the same.

The next time, though, pictures would be taken and the deal would be signed.

Waterman's deal.

And Randall Waterman would make a lot of money.

* * *

Randall Waterman was starving when he arrived in town.

Eddie C's steakhouse looked like the only place open.

He had seen it before, just up the road from the Swiss Cottage Inn where he would stay.

There was also a little adobe Mexican restaurant outside town which looked promising, but by the time Waterman could get there the place would likely have shut for the night.

Eddie C's was also about to close.

The hostess begrudgingly let Waterman sit down and order.

There weren't any other customers in the dining room.

A couple of men came out from the back room laughing. One of the men slapped the other on the back and said something to the woman who had seated Waterman.

She pulled back her fist as if she was going to punch the man then laughed with the men.

"Feisty enough tonight, aren't you, Theresa?"

A tough looking Indian with a black hat and a braid was seated at the bar.

Waterman could see the man. Ronnie Dosela.

Probably Dosela could see Waterman, too from the mirror behind the bar.

Dosela got up, put on a jean jacket, left out the back.

Waterman got a look at him. The picture Irma Dosela kept of her nephew showed a younger man with a basic training haircut.

This was the same guy.

Waterman felt a chill and turned away.

The waitress brought out the steak. Thick and cooked just right with a foil-wrapped potato on the side which Waterman would butter then ignore.

"The guy just left," Waterman said, "you know him?"

"He comes here sometimes," she said. "I wouldn't say I know him."

She was lying, but Waterman didn't care.

"He looked like somebody I know,"

Waterman said. "He looks like a guy works in Old Tucson, making movies. You know his name?"

"Ronnie doesn't make movies," she said. "Not at least any I know about."

She smiled as if one of them had said something funny.

"Ronnie," Waterman said. "Ronnie what?"

"Dosela," she said.

Irma Dosela's nephew.

"You gonna want anything else?" she said.

Waterman looked up at her. She was good looking. Not his type, but nice.

And she had lied about Dosela.

"I don't know," Waterman said. "I might want to think."

"It's just we're closing soon," she said. "You go ahead, though. Don't let me hurry you."

❃ ❃ ❃

Eddie C's was nearly across the street from the motel.

The Swiss Cottage Inn got it's name from the little chalet style cabins.

Waterman banged on the bell at the desk. It was late, but not that damn late.

A woman came out. Maybe forty and wearing jeans and a cable knit sweater.

The woman said room seven was their best.

"We get hunters up here," she said. "You one of them?"

Waterman, still wearing his blazer, chinos and a striped tie couldn't have looked less like a hunter.

Waterman looked at her, searching her face for a trace of sarcasm. She was teasing him. She might as well have called him a city slicker.

"Not me," Waterman said. "I work in finance. High finance."

"There's ice at the end of the hall," she said. She looked at him. "Try keeping it quiet. We like keeping it a nice place."

The room was clean at least.

Wooden paneling and pictures of elk on the wall. A snow capped mountain, possibly Swiss. An ancient television with rabbit ears.

But even located next to the road, the room was quiet.

Waterman couldn't believe the quiet.

He pulled the chain on the door and stepped out of the room. Went down to the ice machine. Returned to the room and poured bourbon over the ice he dropped into a sterilized bathroom glass.

He filled the glass to the bump three quarters of the way up.

Pushed the glass toward his reflection in the bathroom mirror.

"Cheers," he said.

The bottle was still plenty full. Something had caught his attention when he went outside.

Waterman took the glass with him. Unhooked the front door latch again and went out into the cool evening air.

The town was quiet and dark.

Waterman looked up.

Through a canopy formed by the tall ponderosa pines, moonlit clouds drifted in the dark sky.

Their passage revealed a blanket of stars.

He put the tumbler down on the glass topped table next to the door to his motel room.

He went back inside, returning with the full bottle of whiskey and his cigarettes.

❋ ❋ ❋

Waterman didn't have any problem sleeping. Waking up was another story.

Getting out of bed, taking a shower and shaving.

Getting ready for his meeting with the medicine man who nobody said was a medicine man.

What was the guy's name?

Pete Silver.

He would meet Silver at Bashas' parking lot at nine.

Waterman looked at his watch. He had less than an hour to get there. He had no appetite and the whiskey he drank last night made him feel groggy.

Tension in his chest felt like a fist slowly clenching above his diaphragm.

Waterman inhaled. He couldn't let this happen. There was too much at stake today. Meeting could only be a formality unless Mrs. Dosela's vote really was in question.

She was the deciding vote. He needed to do what she said.

He would let the old man show him around the rez.

What the hell? A morning spent with the old man wouldn't kill him.

He looked at the bottle of Ten-High on the dresser and the water glass.

Poured two fingers.

* * *

The clean morning smell of big sagebrush greeted Pete Silver.

He looked at the mountain in the distance. The three mountains were shrouded in clouds. Rain would arrive later in the day, but by then the man from Tucson, Randall Waterman, would be gone. Pete Silver didn't know if he could influence Waterman, but he could try.

He kept the green Coleman camp stove outside near a little patch of brittlebush which had appeared mysteriously a couple of years before.

Morning coffee was boiling water and two big spoons of Nescafe in a blue splatterware cup.

Bacon and eggs in a small cast iron pan sizzled on the other burner.

He felt okay, but he was getting old. He didn't look forward to the events of the upcoming day.

The man from Tucson said he was part Pawnee.

Randall Waterman.

So what? Pete Silver himself had Irish ancestry mixed in with his Apache blood.

Go back long enough, the preacher would tell you, we all go back to Adam and Eve.

Pete had his doubts.

But this Waterman didn't know anything about people. Pete Silver wasn't naive. He knew Waterman wasn't going to change, not with so much money at stake.

But at least Silver could show him something about this place, maybe get through to Waterman in some way.

He could show him the land which would change when the casino was built.

Pete was supposed to meet Waterman in the Bashas' parking lot.

Irma Dosela called him after she spoke to Waterman.

Told him when he should get to the supermarket.

"Don't be late, Pete," she said. "This is important."

Silver looked at his old Datsun pickup. He would take Waterman up to the top of the mountain. Take him up to the ledge and show him the view. Pete Silver didn't take everyone there. Normally wouldn't consider taking Waterman there, even if he *was* part Pawnee. But maybe showing him the vista would give him a chance to talk to the man.

Maybe give Waterman a chance to reconsider the location.

Stranger things had happened.

Pete Silver didn't hold out much hope.

He knew history as well as anyone. And in particular, he knew the history of this place.

The casino would come. The bulldozers would lay open the earth. Already, there were signs up as if the agreement was already in place.

Maybe change was inevitable.

❋ ❋ ❋

Pete Silver waited for Waterman.

Waterman was late.

Bashas' parking lot was filled with vendors. Fry bread. Mutton stew. Mexican blankets strung on clothes lines and waving slowly in the breeze from the red mountain. All the goods were sold from truck tailgates and station wagons circled around the parking lot.

Silver looked around. He knew most of the people here. Mothers and children going in for groceries. Old men like himself standing by the door drinking coffee from Styrofoam cups. Maybe adding something to the coffee, but not making it obvious.

And Waterman hadn't shown up.

Pete Silver went back to his truck to wait. Turned on the radio and listened to the man talking about high school football. Still talking about a game from last year between Blue Ridge and Show Low.

He saw Waterman's Continental coming into the parking lot. A dark blue Lincoln Continental.

A big shot's car.

Silver watched Waterman get out of the car wearing designer jeans and a dress shirt. Blue blazer.

Silver and Waterman shook hands and Silver waved his arm around at the tail-gate merchants.

"Had something for breakfast yet?" he said.

"Thanks," Waterman said. "I don't eat much in the morning. I've never had much of an appetite."

"Your loss," Silver said. "Stew's pretty good right now."

Silver insisted Waterman get into his small truck.

Waterman glanced at the passenger seat then wedged himself into the Datsun.

"Can't get up there in that fancy car of yours," Silver said. "Low as she rides we'd high-bottom for sure. Get stuck in a patch of mud."

Waterman didn't want to get stuck.

* * *

Waterman felt like shit.

Silver had the radio on listening to some kind of Indian chant.

Silver looked at Waterman and turned the radio off.

They sat in the Bashas' parking lot.

Waterman looked out the passenger's side window.

How anyone could oppose bringing any kind of prosperity to this place?

A casino would bring jobs to the community along with the revenue from the gaming.

"You sure you aren't hungry there?"

Waterman realized Silver was talking to him.

"You never tried fry bread up here?" Pete Silver said. "There's nothing like it when it's cooked over mesquite. Beans over the top or honey. You can't beat it."

"Unh-uh," Waterman said.

He felt a knot in his chest the size of his fist. The roiling of his stomach combined with the smell of the tailgaters and Pete Silver's description of the food was beginning to make him sick.

"I'm not really hungry, Mister Silver," he said.

"That's okay, then," Silver said.

He was driving slowly and they were gaining elevation.

"Call me Pete, though. No need for the Mister."

* * *

"We're crossing a pretty important line up here," Pete Silver said. "When you look out over the horizon there, you see part of the town. You can't see it very good today with the clouds."

The elevation was now over seven thousand feet. They had climbed the last twenty minutes through a series of switchbacks overlooking miles of reservation land. The pine trees had thinned out and were replaced by sparse patches of new cedar growth. In the distance, a stand of aspen with their leaves turning yellow.

The Datsun had steadily climbed from the town through the wash and up the mountain. The truck was reliable. Pete Silver never hesitated to drive the truck up here.

The mountain road started to get narrow and then stopped at a wire fence shrouded by bluestem grass. A Masonite sign warned against driving beyond this point.

Pete Silver looked over at Waterman. The man didn't look good.

Sick.

He'd looked bad in the parking lot, but now he looked miserable and his face had a strange cast upon it. He was looking at three little white wooden crosses down the hill from them. The crosses were planted together like a miniature cemetery and Waterman's head was slumped in their direction.

Sometimes altitude would do this, but Silver and Waterman hadn't even gotten close to the top yet.

"We're going to walk now," Pete Silver said. "If you think you can make it."

Waterman stood next to the truck, holding the side view mirror to steady himself.

Early snow lay in patches here at this altitude. It would be gone soon.

"Give me a couple minutes," he said. "I'll be okay."

Pete Silver looked at Waterman. Nodded. Pulled a pack of Kent cigarettes out of his pockets and lighted one.

He watched Waterman. There was something wrong with the man. It wasn't just the elevation, which most people reacted to. This man had a soul-sickness Pete Silver recognized.

There was nothing much left of the road now. It trailed off in two weedy ruts toward a stand of spruce.

Pete Silver looked out from the high peak. No obstructions to their view now. Clouds floated below them and a hawk circled. They stood on a sheer cliff face.

Below them, pine trees.

In the distance, three other mountains.

Beyond those, in the even farther distance,

New Mexico.

He heard Waterman saying something. The man's voice sounded stronger than he would have expected.

"This casino is going to help your people."

Pete Silver looked over the cliff. Patches of early snow hid among the trees. He pointed to a place near the ribbon of road where the gaudy sign had gone up a couple of months before.

The proposed location was barely visible from this height.

"That's the place you want us to build," Silver said.

"Close," Waterman said.

Pete Silver turned to look at Waterman.

"Close," Waterman said again. "Actually, we need your input on placement. You could have a ceremony at the time of ground-breaking and at the time of the actual casino opening."

Silver shook his head.

Waterman wanted Silver to play Indian.

"If the tribe lets you," Pete Silver said. "*If* they let you."

He pulled the leather pouch from the front of his shirt.

* * *

For Ronnie Dosela, tracking the elk was something he'd done all his life. He knew their habits and he knew what would spook them.

Wapiti. He liked the Apache name better than the white man's name for elk.

He stopped and inspected the fresh droppings. From the tracks, Dosela guessed there were two bulls in a band of maybe five or six elk. Hard to say exactly how many. The snow was patchy, but the sun was out. One of those clear fall days you fall in love with. Snow on the ground but you couldn't see your breath. What Dosela could see was an unobstructed view of the valley to the east of the reservation.

Dosela took a Stanley thermos from his pack, unscrewed the top and poured coffee into the silver cup.

He had taken his rifle from his truck, but Dosela wasn't hunting yet. He was scouting. He would come back in a few days to take his elk.

Dosela rested on his haunches, coffee to his side, looking through binoculars at the valley.

Cattle moved across the range. It had been a dry summer and the cattle were skinny.

Things were going to change here. The casino would change things for sure.

This place would never be the same.

He put the top back on the thermos jug. Climbed back to his feet and started walking farther up the road. He was near the place where the road ended.

He saw the truck.

There were plenty of Datsun pickups on the rez. Plenty of them, but only one of them was Pete

Silver's.

Dosela knew the tan truck by sight.

He felt a drop of rain and then seconds later another one. Dosela looked at the dark sky.

Saw a flash of lightning cross the sky. He counted until he heard the thunder. The storm was probably up north of here.

Pete Silver would be up above the tree line tending to the Crown Dancer shrines. Dosela would wait for Pete Silver from a respectful distance. There were matters of ritual Pete Silver could perform but Dosela could not.

Dosela liked Pete Silver, though.

Dosela thought about the Crown Dancers and the dance. He had been away for a long time and remembered sometimes waking up in the barracks in Germany remembering the ceremonies which took place on this mountain.

Pete Silver was out here somewhere, and Dosela would wait for him out of courtesy for an elder.

He leaned against the older man's truck and rolled a cigarette.

❈ ❈ ❈

Randall Waterman watched Pete Silver take the leather pouch from his neck and hold it in his hands.

Silver stood next to Waterman, near the

edge of the cliff. He started to sing.

Silver's voice sounded guttural and emotional. The strange syllables increased Waterman's unease.

Pete Silver poured ground corn from his pouch into the palm of his creased right hand.

Waterman felt his pulse starting to race. The tightness in his chest increased. He was going to have to do something.

Pete Silver's voice started to raise. The syllables blended.

Waterman began to feel as if he understood their meaning.

He had to be dreaming.

He felt disoriented.

Waterman needed to do something quickly. He remembered the meditative technique from the seminar.

He needed time. Time to think things over.

Jabbing pain hit Waterman's chest. He held his breath.

Disassociate.

Waterman's thoughts shifted from his head to somewhere above his body. He wasn't *really* here on top of this mountain. He was high above the ground now, somewhere in the clouds.

He dropped to his knees, holding his hands to his chest.

Waterman gasped for breath.

Detach.

Waterman panicked.

This was an illusion. He wasn't really here.

He saw the look of panic on the old man's face. Saw him drop the open pouch. Watched the remaining cornmeal fall to the ground.

Depart.

Waterman forced himself to his knees and then to his feet. He staggered toward Pete Silver and grasped the collar of the old man's jacket. Started to tug.

Pete Silver tried to keep Waterman from falling.

Silver held the younger man in order to keep both of them from plummeting into the abyss.

They stood on top of the mountain, held together in a fierce dance.

Waterman felt himself violently turn. Felt himself loosening his grip on the old man's collar. Waterman let go.

The older man reeled, staggered, tried to stop himself. Momentum carried the old man over the cliff's edge.

❊ ❊ ❊

Waterman forced himself up to his knees.

He lay on the ground for some time. How long, he wasn't certain.

He worked his way over to the edge and looked down. There was no sign of where Pete Silver had landed, there were only rocks.

Waterman felt his chest. His breathing was

back to normal. Whatever had come over him had ended quickly.

A panic attack. He had experienced them before.

The old man must have thought Waterman was having a heart attack. If he hadn't grabbed Waterman, Pete Silver wouldn't have fallen.

The pouch with the remaining grains of the cornmeal lay near the edge of the cliff. Waterman glanced at it, then kicked at the thing with the toe of his shoe.

Watched the pouch drop over the cliff.

He turned away and started down the mountain path toward Pete Silver's truck. Already, Waterman was forming the outline of the story he would have to tell when he got back to town in Pete Silver's Datsun.

The day had been wonderful, Waterman would say.

Wonderful at least, until the unexpected and tragic event occurred. Pete Silver explained so much to Waterman while they were on top of the mountain. Silver detailed his hopes for the casino. He talked at length about his high hopes for the good things the revenue from the gaming could produce for his people.

Waterman smiled.

It would be simple. Although the old man's death had been unfortunate, it made the completion of the deal less complicated.

* * *

Waterman stumbled down the trail.

He repeated the story to himself, emphasizing the way the old man clasped his hands on his chest before falling over the cliff.

Heart attack.

Nobody was going to question him, were they?

Silver was an old man.

Waterman kicked at the red cinders on the trail.

His tassel loafers were a mess. He shouldn't have worn them.

It had to be getting close to noon. He was tired and now he felt a little hungry.

He had to be getting close to Pete Silver's truck. Fortunately, the old man left his keys in the ignition. Waterman would drive the truck down from the mountain.

Probably his best choice would be to go immediately to Tribal Headquarters.

Or should he go to the hospital?

The emergency room?

Police station?

He wasn't sure.

He saw Pete Silver's tan Datsun in the distance.

The man standing next to the truck looked familiar.

A big man with a black hat holding a rifle and smoking a cigarette.

* * *

Waterman told Dosela the story he had rehearsed while stumbling down the trail.

Dosela looked at Waterman

"Pete Silver's still up there?"

Waterman shook his head.

Pointed.

"He has to be down there somewhere. I couldn't see him."

* * *

Dosela nodded.

Waterman's shoes were muddy, but his clothes were otherwise spotless.

"You didn't look for him, then?"

Waterman held out his hands palms-up.

"I thought the best thing I could do was to get help. In town."

Dosela squinted.

"I'm your help."

* * *

He didn't have a pulse.

Ronnie Dosela placed Pete Silver's hands on

top of the old man's faded Levi jacket.

He didn't know the proper ritual. Somebody else would. Anyway, Dosela wasn't concerned with that.

"You were going to leave him out here," he said.

Waterman was having a hard time breathing. His face was flushed and he stooped over slightly. He didn't look at Pete Silver's body. He put up his right hand in the stop sign.

Breathing heavily and shaking his head.

Waterman's clothes were dirty now. Pete Silver's body had not been easy to find in the brush. The arm of Waterman's coat was ripped and mud covered his lower legs.

"I wasn't sure what to do," he said.

Dosela nodded.

"We're taking him home," Dosela said. "Grab under his arm."

* * *

Dosela took two blankets from behind the front seat of Pete Silver's Datsun and laid them in the bed of the truck.

While Waterman watched, Dosela took a hunting knife from his belt, cut several cedar branches from nearby bushes, and put them around the body of Pete Silver.

Dosela had already sized up Waterman.

Tracking elk had taught Dosela a lot. A good

tracker used all of his senses. Sight and sound were just the start.

Dosela's olfactory sense had been refined over the years.

Just like elk, men gave off different kinds of odors. There was a difference, for example, between the smell of rutting and the smell of fear.

Dosela smelled fear on this man's body.

Dosela got behind the wheel of the truck and took the keys from under the visor on the driver's side.

Started the truck and looked at Waterman who huddled on the passenger side.

Waterman was shivering.

"It doesn't matter what you tell the people in town," Dosela said. "You're going to tell me the truth about what happened up there. Do you hear me?"

Waterman nodded.

* * *

He had nothing to hide.

Waterman looked at Dosela. They were at the police station. Dosela had already shown the police Pete Silver's body.

Waterman had felt Dosela watching him. Waiting for Waterman to trip up and say something incriminating.

"He was having some kind of an attack," Waterman said. "I tried to keep him away from the edge, but I couldn't."

Waterman put his head into his hands. Listened.

There was nothing more to be done. Pete Silver's death had been a terrible accident.

There would be an inquest, of course, but there was no reason for Waterman to stay if he had no more business in the town.

Waterman didn't want to ask for a ride. Even though the rain was coming down hard now, Bashas wasn't far from the station.

He tried to put out of his mind the look Pete Silver had on his face before falling off the cliff.

And he also tried to put out of mind the look Dosela gave him when he left the police station.

He tried to think of other things. There was no obstacle now to building the casino.

They would sign the paperwork later in the week.

But Waterman couldn't escape the look Dosela gave him when he left.

Dosela's look was hard and unforgiving.

TWO COWBOYS STANDING WITH HORSES IN A SMALL INDIAN VILLAGE

Middle of the day felt too late to go to the Western Way to Frank Trinity.

Even in the foothills, Tucson's heat hadn't subsided yet but Millie Parsons had called and said she had a court reserved for one o'clock and Frank would be an absolute darling if he could come up and help her with a hitch in her backhand which was driving her crazy.

Who could turn Millie Parsons down?

Millie had been married twice to Phil Parsons. Millie and Phil had been divorced the first time around, and now Phil was dead.

Trinity had done some work for Phil Parsons.

Millie was in her forties. A woman who could have gotten by on her looks, but didn't. A nice woman who played a decent game of tennis.

Trinity checked his empty schedule for the day, looked around for his whites, then tossed his wooden Davis racket into the back of the Bronco.

He headed out of the Presidio through downtown and Fourth Avenue to Miracle Mile until it turned into Oracle then followed the curves to the Western Way.

Swimming pools, movie stars.

The old dude ranch made him feel like Gary Cooper heading for a date with his old childhood friend Myrna Loy.

He saw Millie's yellow Mercedes in the parking lot. Millie was on the court already warming up.

Millie looked as good as a bereaved widow possibly could in a pleated white tennis skirt and sleeveless top.

Trinity had been playing tennis with Millie for a while.

She had referred a case to Trinity once.

Something about Phil's ex-wife, the second one.

To her credit, Millie never inquired about the outcome.

It was just her backhand causing problems. Millie had just enough of a hitch in her stroke to throw her motion off. The problem couldn't be seen unless you were looking for it, and Trinity wasn't looking.

They played just long enough to forget about the backhand.

Afterward, they sat near the court drinking Perrier.

Millie lighted a cigarette.

"I shouldn't," she said, cupping the cigarette as if there was a breeze.

"Maybe you should use both hands, like Chris Evert," Trinity said.

"Aren't you clever?" she said. "As if I haven't tried that a hundred and ten times."

"I'm not a tennis coach," Trinity said. "I'm just a recreational player."

She looked at him. Laughed.

"I suppose you put that on your tax return, Frank? Recreational tennis player?"

"Something like that," he said. "It varies from year to year. I haven't gotten into a pattern yet."

She exhaled. Paused.

"I'll just bet."

The two men on the court now were serious corporate types, slinging their rackets with authority.

The man on the far court was the kind of player who Trinity liked to play for money. The kind of player with deep pockets and well-developed hubris.

Sure of his skilled, mono-dimensional game and the advantage he gained using the latest in high-tech rackets.

Trinity watched the men duel in the sun. He could beat either of the men handily even with his wooden Davis.

Millie was saying something to Trinity.

She was saying something about a green carpet and getting some artwork in her house appraised.

"Just to get an idea, Frank. Not that I'm selling."

He definitely wasn't listening.

She puffed her cigarette then ground it out into the glass ashtray.

"Can't hurt to find out what things are worth, right Frank?"

Trinity looked at her. She was waiting for an answer.

"Of course not, Millie," Trinity said. "I think you're being smart."

"You should come up sometime, Frank. I mean it. You should."

Trinity nodded.

Looked at Millie.

"Invite me sometime. We'll see what happens."

❋ ❋ ❋

"That's it then?" Millie Parsons said.

She was in her foothills home talking to her lawyer on the telephone.

"That's the long and the short of it," Joe Sawyer said.

She heard him sniff.

"You could be looking at a fairly long wait, Millie. I don't know how else to put it to you. I wish I had better news but I don't."

Millie put the phone down and looked at the carpet. So much for the feeling of well-being the tennis date with Frank Trinity had accomplished. She felt lousy again. The calls she made to her lawyer were accomplishing nothing except adding to his billable hours, a point Sawyer had made more than once.

"Especially after hours," Sawyer said. "I have my girl pay special attention to calls after nine. She's locked into a particular way of doing things and I can't do anything about it without causing a ruckus you wouldn't want to see. Why not call back in the morning?"

His girl.

Millie had never seen anyone in Sawyer's office except Sawyer.

Millie shook her head. Mornings were different. When the sun came up, she didn't feel the darkness caving in on her. Oh well, so she was being *dramatic*. But why shouldn't she be a little dramatic? She had every reason.

Anyway, Millie never felt the need to call in the mornings.

It was already dark and when she looked out the plate glass window, she saw clouds in the dark sky, drifting past the Catalinas. Better to focus on the inside of the house and on the carpet.

Phil's carpet was green, and it stretched from the open kitchen to a white leather couch near an enormous fireplace.

The night sky over Tucson, visible from the floor to ceiling windows in the foothills house was the purple shade which followed sunset.

Millie Parsons had turned on every light she could find and the inside of the house was bright. The living room looked like a little theater set with Millie Parsons standing at center stage, holding a cigarette in her extended right hand, waiting for the leading man to come on stage.

Oh say, Millie. Up rather late aren't we?

* * *

You could practice a short golf game on the green rug.

Phil Parsons used to do exactly that, leaning over his putter, letting what was left of his hair fall down into his eyes. The carpet would have been better suited to a law office or a men's locker room than it was to the first floor of the foothills home of the late Phil Parsons, but you couldn't have told that to Phil.

You really couldn't tell very much to Phil.

Millie Parsons would never have chosen the

carpeting. Not for a second. Millie's tastes were up-to-the-minute. The wall-to-wall looked so obvious and unimaginative to Millie. It was the first item on her definitely-must-change list now that she was the soon-to-be-sole owner of the house.

Phil Parsons insisted on the carpet's color when he and Millie remarried. He bought it at store with a neon sign in the shape of enormous genie in front.

The Magic Carpet. Phil laughed about the sign and laughed telling Millie about the guy who owned the place.

"Sam Koory," he said, "Sam's a Lebanese guy just about five foot nothing. He bought the sign at an auction in Yuma and strapped it to the roof of his car to bring it back to 22nd Street. The Magic Carpet. I asked him why he didn't just take a truck down there, he's got all these trucks for the carpets? Know what he said?"

Millie shook her head.

"Unh-uh."

"Honest to God, Sam is such a character. Sam figures the genie's got so much luck, he can't take the chance to wait and bring it up later. Like even just the amount of time it takes to get one of his trucks down there. Sam figures the genie's gonna make sales for him, and he doesn't want to jinx it. I hate to tell Sam the sign's got nothing to do with it. Because he was as proud of the thing as anything. I got the impression if I'd asked him to, Sam would have brought his sales figures out from before and after he bought the sign."

"You really got into all this with the guy?" Millie said. "Was this before or after you bought the carpet?"

Phil looked at her.

"Before, during, after? Who knows? It was all he could talk about, and it's not like this genie just went up. It's been there at least a couple years."

"Maybe more than that," Millie said. "I've seen it. It's been up there for years."

"You gotta admit it catches your attention," Phil said. "I must have driven by the place a hundred times and I never made the connection it was a place to buy a carpet. Even with the name."

"You bought a carpet from him," Millie said. "Isn't it possible the genie influenced your decision, even in the teensiest way? Subliminally?"

"That's not the way subliminal advertising works," Phil said.

Laughing.

Before, Phil would have gotten upset. This time, he looked at Millie as if she had just said something exceptionally cute. He wasn't hard to figure out, if you knew him for a while. Millie, having been married to him twice, knew Phil as well as anyone knew him.

The color of the carpet seemed like a small concession to Millie at the time.

Millie humored Phil. It was her strategy to survive their second marriage.

"This carpet looks like money," Phil said.

"Green and gold attract wealth, Millie. That's something Sam Koory doesn't know. You can bet your bottom dollar on that. A lot of people don't know that. They stay broke and they never figure out why. A rug like this speaks of wealth and attraction."

To Millie, the size and shade of the carpet spoke more of miniature golf than money.

Phil was dead now, and in spite of everything, Millie missed him.

He had suffered a sudden heart attack in bed and long before the emergency personnel arrived, Millie knew he was gone.

She'd watched him being taken from the house and a strange ambivalent feeling came over her which she knew would take time to sort out.

Whatever her feelings were, Millie was very much alive and would now own the house and all the rest of Phil's estate.

Eventually anyway.

Phil died shortly after he and Millie had remarried. Their first wedding had been traditional. The second had been held in back of this house with the spectacular view of the Catalina Mountains behind Millie, Phil, and the minister.

Phil's death was a shock to Millie.

Millie would be wealthy once all the settlements were made. Of course, with Phil's multiple marriages, the estate was complicated.

Millie had been Phil's first wife and then

after a period of time, his last. She would be well taken care of.

There was only one problem, and it embarrassed Millie.

During the time they were divorced, Phil's payments to Millie had been generous and dependable. She had lived a more than comfortable life.

Tennis.

Salon treatments at the Western Way.

Travel.

Clothing.

The yellow Mercedes.

Except Millie had put nothing away.

When Phil asked her to marry him again, Millie had considered her options.

Phil was the one who wanted the divorce in the first place. Their divorce started the odyssey of Phil's two subsequent marriages. Millie had watched from the sidelines. Phil would call her and she would listen to him reciting the problems with his current wife.

Both of Phil's wives were younger than Millie. Much younger, if she was honest, but no one could say they were more beautiful than Millie.

That was a fact. An objective statement.

It was not the opinion of a vain woman.

Millie was not vain.

The problem, bluntly, was Millie was currently cash poor.

Everything would be fine once the estate

settled, but Joe Sawyer said finalizing the proceedings could take months, not weeks.

No more than six months, Joe Sawyer said.

In the meantime, Millie needed money.

And that was where Jorge Alonso came in.

Millie knew Jorge well enough to call him. He had come up to her house, and when she visited his shop Jorge greeted her as if they were best friends.

Jorge could look at Phil's collection of paintings.

If she could sell one or two of them discretely, her problems would be solved.

Phil had spent a fortune on these paintings.

Millie had a stack of bills to pay. She liked her way of life. She didn't want to change it while Joe Sawyer crawled at the pace of a snail through the estate proceedings.

She needed money. Not a fortune. Just something to tide her over. Keep the coyotes at bay.

Phil's estate included financial holdings all over the southwest.

The scope of his estate was well beyond Millie's attorney Joe Sawyer's abilities. Sawyer told her so.

"I'm telling you, Millie," Sawyer said, "I gotta ham and eggs practice here. Your occasional filet mignon, but this ain't one of those. It *coulda* been, if Phil had something reasonable drawn up, but he didn't."

Sawyer referred Millie to a team of

specialists who he assured Millie would get the job done as quickly as possible.

"They'll get your money for you, Millie," Sawyer said. "They're pros. You gotta be patient though. Rome wasn't built in a day."

Millie had been younger than Phil when they married the first time.

She joked that she felt *much* younger than Phil on the occasion of their second marriage.

Phil Parsons appreciated her more the second time around.

"How about this?" Phil said. "I hit the jackpot twice in my life. Maybe I'll smarten up this time."

Marrying Phil for the second time brought rewards. Millie looked around the walls of the living room. In this room, and through the entire house, Phil's collection of art dominated the walls.

Abstract paintings and sculpture.

Millie had no idea how much it was all worth, but she was going to talk to Jorge Alonso.

Jorge would be here tomorrow morning and he would look at the collection.

Jorge was honest, he dealt in Native American jewelry and artifacts.

Millie trusted Jorge.

Phil Parsons hadn't trusted anyone. Not with finances, anyway. Millie would be glad to find out what the artwork was really worth.

And if the price was right, Millie just might be persuaded to part with some of the pieces.

Despite what some thought, Millie had

struggled with her decision to remarry Phil.

He hadn't fussed over the generous monthly maintenance Joe Sawyer had negotiated for her.

"Why should he?" Sawyer said. "It's chump change for him, Millie."

And between their marriages, conversations between Phil and Millie had always been civil.

Millie had met the two women Phil had married and listened to his laments after both women left him.

They had a cordial relationship which Millie hadn't expected would change.

Then, out of the blue, Phil decided what he really wanted to do was to remarry Millie.

Jorge laughed when Millie told him about Phil's proposal.

"He's trying to recapture his youth, honey," Jorge said. "It's a machismo thing."

His reasons didn't matter to Millie.

And everybody who knew him knew that when Phil Parsons decided upon something, he wouldn't be deterred.

Phil had announced that the house in the foothills of the Catalinas was his wedding present to Millie.

Only after his death was Millie told that there could be complications in the will.

She would have to wait to see what happened in probate.

But in the meantime, she could enjoy living in the house as long as she changed nothing.

She was free to enjoy this architectural marvel overlooking the diamond necklace of Tucson's nighttime skyline.

She could enjoy Phil's collection of modern art.

And she could enjoy the living room's enormous emerald green wall to wall carpeting.

She just couldn't change it.

❊ ❊ ❊

Millie Parsons liked Jorge Alonso.

She liked his dark, handsome looks and she liked the way he wore a paisley kerchief around his neck which made him look like Ricardo Montalbán in the years before he landed on Fantasy Island. Jorge was just as handsome as Ricardo Montalbán, but Millie didn't need to worry about the complications of romance with Jorge. Women didn't interest Jorge.

And Jorge seemed to know something about everything. Millie could talk about anything with Jorge without worrying about his motives. Everything was uncomplicated with Jorge and Millie trusted him.

Jorge, holding the teacup Millie gave him, sniffed at the abstracts on the living room walls. They were big canvases. Each of them about five feet high. Splashy and loud.

"Nothing, Millie. Absolutely nada." he said. "They're interesting, all right, but no value. I could have my friend look at them, but I wouldn't get your hopes up."

Jorge's friend.

Millie could imagine Jorge's friend. Probably very much like Jorge. A sharp-dressed small man holding his teacup just so.

Paintings weren't Jorge's specialty. Jorge dealt in Native American artifacts and jewelry but Millie hoped he could at least give her an idea of the value of the paintings. The paintings had been painted by David Lawrence, a Bisbee artist. Phil's last wife had left Phil for Lawrence, but Phil didn't hold it against the artist.

"It could have been anyone," Phil said. "It just happened to be this artist. I never held it against him. Plus, I like the paintings and they were a good investment."

Phil was pragmatic.

"Being married to that one was like keeping a firefly in a glass jar."

Jorge had taken several steps back from the abstracts and looked at them with studied indifference.

"Never heard of him," Jorge said when Millie mentioned Lawrence's name. "The name David Lawrence means literally nothing to me. Should it?"

"I don't know," Millie said. "That's what I want to find out."

Jorge turned his from from the living room and peeked into Phil's study.

"Everything's insured, isn't it?" Jorge said. "There *have* been break-ins."

Of course everything had been insured. Phil was careful.

"There's nothing in there," Millie said, "that's just Phil's study."

Jorge had already gone into the room, straight to the far wall.

He was looking at the small painting over Phil's desk.

More than looking at it. He was staring.

Millie hadn't looked at Phil's desk since he died and she'd barely looked at it before. The painting meant very little to her. She was thinking about the gun.

He had once opened the polished mahogany desk to show her the gun he kept inside.

If it was valuable, she should show Jorge. It wasn't any use to her.

Phil had shown Millie the revolver, saying he wanted her to know it was there.

"It's a Smith and Wesson 44, Millie," Phil had said. "One of the Russian models. They made them for one of the czars. Accurate as hell and packs a punch."

Phil held the revolver up to show Millie, pointed to the cylinder, which was loaded.

"Works just like your domestic models," Phil said. "It has a few Russki modifications. This spur under the trigger, for one. God knows what they were thinking."

"Why are you showing me this?"

"Just so you know where it is, Millie," Phil said. "You're my wife, aren't you? You never know what can happen when I'm not on the scene."

Millie shook her head.

"Here," Phil said, "I'll show you how to load this."

"I know how to load a gun, Phil. I'm not completely helpless."

Phil put the revolver back in the drawer and Millie had forgotten about it just like she'd forgotten about the western painting Jorge was now examining.

Millie had never looked at the painting closely. It was part of the landscape of Phil's office as far as she was concerned.

Two cowboys standing with horses in a small Indian village.

It was well done, she supposed. If she *had* to offer an opinion. The painting was not Millie's cup of tea. She liked the abstract paintings better.

Jorge was looking closely at the painting. He took out a magnifying glass from a leather case in his pocket and examined the bottom right hand corner.

Jorge turned to Millie.

"Is there any more light in here?"

She turned the dimmer switch clockwise. Phil liked the room to be dark. He conducted most of his business at his office and kept this study dark and unoccupied.

This study was just a showcase and Millie never went into it.

"What are you looking at, Jorge?"

"I'm not sure, Millie. It's not my area." He turned away from the smaller painting. You know what? I could be wrong about the abstracts. I'd like to have my friend take a look."

Millie stood next to Jorge. Looking at him closely.

"If any of them are valuable, I wouldn't necessarily be opposed to selling," she said.

Jorge nodded. He stepped away from the painting of the cowboys.

"I'll call my friend," Jorge said. "He knows these things better than anyone."

Millie nodded.

Jorge's friend.

Jorge looked at her.

"You can trust him."

"There's a gun in the desk," Millie said. "Phil treated it like it was something special. He said it's Russian. Open the drawer."

Jorge pulled the center drawer open and glanced in the desk. Took the gun out of the drawer and held it up with the barrel pointed toward the ceiling. He examined it, looking carefully at the additional flange under the trigger guard and the knob behind the grip.

"Unusual," he said. "Cyrillic. Russian, like you said. We can have him take a look at this, too. He'll know about it."

Jorge placed the gun back in the drawer.

"Any particular reason you keep it loaded?" he said.

She hadn't loaded the gun. She couldn't remember even touching it. But why would Phil keep an unloaded gun in his desk?

Phil would have gone into his *Shane* routine, if she had asked.

A gun is just a tool, Millie. As good or as bad as the man using it.

"I don't know," Millie said. "I never touched Phil's things. I still don't. I do know how to shoot, though."

Jorge laughed.

"I thought at first you were talking about a dueling piece. This really does have a very commanding presence. You want me to take the bullets out?"

Millie shrugged.

"I know how. I'm not completely defenseless.

She paused.

"Do you think it's worth something?"

"We'll have my friend look at it," Jorge said. "If there's one thing he knows, it's guns."

* * *

Three days passed without Jorge calling.

Millie had given up on calling Joe Sawyer back. What was the point of calling him?

Sawyer only told Millie to be patient.

Millie tried to be patient, but she knew there was a limit.

* * *

Jorge was busy. He'd been thinking. Ever since he'd seen the painting.

He hoped Millie hadn't noticed his interest in the painting. He'd tried to move her attention back to the ridiculous abstracts. And then there had been all that business about the gun.

Standing in his living room, Jorge held the phone in one hand.

In his other hand he held a mimosa.

It was evening, but mimosas were Jorge's signature drink.

He pursed his lips, listening to the man on the other end of the line.

"The provenance is complicated Billy. Let's just say that."

There was silence on the other end of the line.

"So, you aren't going to tell me, am I right?"

Jorge shook his head.

"That's not at all what I'm saying. I'm just saying it's complicated and I don't want to get into it with you at this point. What I need to know is if you're interested. You'd be a fool not to be at least a tiny bit interested. The painting is worth a fortune. You know it is. And I can get the painting for nothing."

"Uh huh. You can get it."

"I definitely can," Jorge said.

"Meaning you don't have it. You get the thing, I'll take a look at it. I won't promise anything though."

"You're a stickler, aren't you?"

"Damn right I am. Show me where it comes from, I'm interested. Otherwise I'll pass. I've seen fakes out there. So have you. They're a dime a dozen."

It was Jorge's turn to go silent. Not for long.

"This is the real thing. I couldn't believe it when I saw it. It's a couple cowboys and some horses. You're going to love it."

"A couple of cowboys, huh?"

"And horses," Jorge said.

"Horses, right. You told me that. We'll see."

* * *

Millie always kept the casement windows open at night. Just slightly. Millie didn't like the feel of unrelenting air conditioned air. Of course when Phil was alive, he required all the rooms to be set to 67 degrees and he'd given Millie hell about open windows.

"This house is climate controlled," he said. "It's delicate, dammit and it has a mind of it's own. You mess with it, the air conditioning starts to think 'these people got no idea how to operate this' and it starts to go all haywire."

She would change the system in the house as soon as she could. She liked the feeling of real air circulating from open windows and she didn't mind a little heat.

Millie wasn't going to bed yet. She was thinking.

As soon as she had the money she would change a lot of things in the house.

If Sawyer would just get the estate settled.

In the meantime, the window and the sliding door to the back patio were both open. Only a screen between Millie and the outside world.

During the day, Millie liked sitting on the patio, watching quails and hummingbirds. When evening came she watched the sunsets.

She had turned the lights down, and sat in front of the fireplace.

The place was romantic, Phil had gotten that part right.

She stood up and went to Phil's study.

The gun was still in his desk. Something about being alone in the big house had started to feel uncomfortable a day or two ago and she had looked at the revolver again.

The gun was large and heavy in her hand and looked particularly dangerous in half-light. She wondered about the faint line of Cyrillic characters. Phil would have known what they meant and he would have been happy to tell her.

The phone rang. Jorge. Finally.

"He's absolutely the best at what he does, Millie. Take it from me. He's the best. End of story. And he's handsome in a rugged kind of way. You would adore him."

"That's nice, Jorge. Does that mean I'm not meeting him?"

"Sorry, Millie. I'd love to have you meet him, but no-can-do. He's not available. I gave him a good description of the Lawrence paintings, though. He's *very* interested."

"Can he come another time?"

"Oh sure," Jorge said. "Of course."

"Well that's something, anyway."

"Right," he said. "It's something."

"Sorry," he said.

"Look," he said. "About the cowboy painting. How about I come up tomorrow and I'll..."

"I don't think so," she said. "I don't think I want to sell."

"You're sure?" Jorge said. "I might be able get you a good price for it."

"I'm sure, she said.

Millie looked out at the living room.

The light from the moon created shadows on the cholla cactus outside and a beam cast through the window to the fireplace. There were seven mesquite logs in the fireplace. Matchsticks and pine heartwood kindling.

Her bedroom door was open.

❉ ❉ ❉

The phone call surprised Trinity. It wasn't late, but it wasn't early, either. He answered it before the machine took over. A woman's voice. At first, Trinity couldn't tell who was speaking.

"This is Millie, Frank," she said.

Had it been three days or four since their last game of tennis at the Westward Way?

"Frank, I know it's late. I'm sorry, but is it too late to talk to you? You said I should invite you. Can I see you?"

"What's this about, Millie?" Trinity said.

"Frank," she said, "It's not about anything. I'm inviting you."

Trinity glanced at the clock.

Nine thirty. Not too late. Not too late at all.

"I'd like to see you," she said. "It doesn't have to be tennis."

"Tonight?" he said.

❊ ❊ ❊

She met him at the front door.

Trinity had taken a shower and tugged on his boots and put on a lightweight sport coat over jeans and an oxford cloth shirt. Millie leaned forward and they kissed. Trinity hadn't kissed her before. The kiss was nice.

"You've never seen my house," she said. "Come in."

She showed him the house.

Millie showed Trinity the abstracts and the

sculptures in the living room. She showed him the painting of the cowboys Jorge had tried hard not to show interest in.

* * *

They were in the living room looking out over the lights of Tucson.

"Honestly Frank," Millie said. "He was practically drooling over the thing. Then he started to act like it wasn't worth anything at all. I'm not a fool. It's not my favorite, but I know it's valuable."

Trinity had lighted the mesquite logs in the fireplace.

Millie was in his arms.

He nodded.

"Funny kind of reaction he had looking at it."

"Yes" she said, "funny."

TEN SHOTS QUICK

When Jackie Fuller, twenty-eight, took the phone call from Jorge Alonso she had just gone to bed and was in the half-world you sometimes reach seconds before sleep.

Jackie picked up the phone on the third ring, pushing aside the Savage .32 semi-automatic she kept on her nightstand. A call from Jorge Alonso meant Jackie was going to kill somebody.

That was what a call from Jorge meant.

Jackie looked like a young Elizabeth Montgomery holding the blue princess phone.

"Jackie, you need to get up here. I have something *very big* for you."

Jorge, always breathless. Impatient.

But Jorge wasn't unpredictable.

She hadn't sought Jorge out to get in this line of work, but she hadn't turned it down when offered.

"That's you, Jorge?" Jackie said. She pulled the sheet up and around herself.

Satin, a luxurious choice she'd made on the spur of the moment, just like her decision to rent this townhouse. She had read about satin sheets in one of the novels she liked and had wondered if they were as sleek as they sounded.

They were.

Now, Jackie wouldn't have any other kind.

She had made a mistake and turned the air conditioning down too low. She felt a chill.

"Just get up here as quickly as you can," Jorge said. "This job is good. *More* than good. Time is of the essence."

Jackie turned on the bedside lamp and placed her feet on the carpet.

When was time not of the essence with Jorge Alonso?

She would cut down Tucson Boulevard and be there as quickly as she needed to be. If the job was big, Jorge needed her more than she needed him.

"Mmm-hmm," she said. "I'm on my way, Jorge."

❉ ❉ ❉

"It took you long enough," he said.

"I'm supposed to jump out of bed and be here just like that, Jorge?"

Jorge shook his head.

"I could get somebody else, you know."

"No you couldn't," Jackie said. "We both

know that."

Jorge Alonso, dressed in a two-toned smoking jacket sat in front of Jackie.

He was drinking an iced mimosa from a long-stemmed crystal wine glass.

His living room illuminated by candles.

He offered a mimosa to Jackie but she shook her head no.

Jorge and his mimosas. All day long and into the night.

"The guy you meet is giving you the money. You're meeting him there tomorrow night. Albuquerque is what, six hours?" Jorge surveyed Jackie's face.

"Seven, Jorge. I might want to stop somewhere. Get something to eat. Stretch my legs."

Jorge ignored her.

"And that's *all* he's going to do for you. This guy knows *nothing*. Which is just as well. I'm giving you everything for instructions. Your man will be exactly where I tell you he is."

Jackie nodded.

"Don't let him give you any of the old 'what's-a-nice-girl-like-you?' crap, either."

Jackie rolled her eyes. Took out a cigarette and a pack of paper matches.

Jorge always insisted the less Jackie knew the better.

Albuquerque?

"This guy, Jorge. The one I'm meeting. Why

is he involved anyway?"

She was giving Jorge a hard time. Letting him splutter around like a hooked fish. She already knew the answer.

"Ours is not to question why, sweetie," Jorge said. He finished the mimosa and fished a cherry from the glass, holding the stem between his thumb and index finger. Inspecting the surface.

"This is the way they want it and this is the way they get it."

Jorge had thrown out a big figure this time.

More than usual.

If she took the job, Jackie would be set for months and she could enjoy the townhouse. Get it painted, maybe. She had bought some design magazines and given colors some thought.

Something bold. Anything but the Navajo white already on the walls.

Jorge Alonso described the second man to Jackie. Not the contact. Not the guy giving her the money.

Jackie needed to memorize the details about the man Jorge Alonso described to her. This was the man in Jackie's crosshairs.

Jorge described the car the man drove and Jackie memorized the license plate numbers.

Jorge was a fussy man, a dapper dresser. An antique collector. His clients knew him as a man who got things done.

"Still using the same gun, sweetie?" Jorge said.

Jackie looked at him. Why would she change? Jorge made it sound like she was wearing last year's fashion.

Jackie usually kept the Savage .32 semi-automatic in her shoulder bag. She had the gun with her now. Jorge had given it to her in the first place, hadn't he? Jorge, who bought and sold Indian jewelry said he had taken the gun in on a trade.

Jackie hadn't known very much about guns when he gave it to her. One was the same as the other to her.

"Of course, Jorge. You aren't thinking about taking it back are you?"

"That gun doesn't even exist," Jorge said. "I don't want to talk about it. Why are you even talking about it?"

Jorge was like that. He'd bring up a subject and then he would clam up about it just as quickly.

She wasn't going to give up this gun or use any other. There wasn't any reason to do so.

Jorge was right. The gun *was* clean. No numbers or marks on the barrel. It didn't exist.

Jorge *said* he had taken it in trade, but she wondered.

Jackie liked the way the vintage firearm felt in her hand.

Ten shots quick.

Savage's company slogan made Jackie laugh. Who needs ten shots?

The Savage had plenty of stopping power for

her purposes. More than enough.

She wasn't going to indulge in any gun debates, either.

She wasn't hunting for big game.

The .32 was fine because Jackie knew what she was doing at short range.

She kept the Savage clean, easily within reach, and out of sight.

She was ready for the job.

* * *

Wearing a dark wig, black skirt, and white blouse, Jackie ordered a screwdriver from the blonde barmaid in the dark Ramada Inn outside Albuquerque.

Jorge Alonso suggested the clothing, and Jackie had to admit it was a good idea. All except the padded shoulders which were ridiculous.

"It's camouflage, sweetie," Jorge said. "Just think of it like camouflage. You want to blend into the landscape."

Teasing her. Like the electric blue Impala wouldn't be noticed.

"For this job, you're a corporate girl on her way up. Hide in plain sight."

"This is Albuquerque, right? Shouldn't I be wearing Ropers?"

"It's the new west, Jackie. Get with the times."

Jackie looked at the barmaid who also wore a

black skirt and white blouse. Both were tighter on the blonde, but nevertheless, the two women were dressed the same.

So much for corporate camouflage. Jorge wanted her to dress like a cocktail waitress.

Jackie had driven straight north from Tucson passing Picacho, Casa Grande, Phoenix on her way to Albuquerque. Using a Florida drivers license Jorge gave her for identification.

The Rent-a-Wreck Impala paid for with a Diner's Club in the same name. The rented car was fast but she kept it under seventy most of the way, especially in the speed trap past Black Canyon City.

Jorge Alonso had given her the hurry-up identification with a flourish. Jackie's picture with a Joan Jett scowl on her face.

The name on the license was Jill Miller.

"Jill Miller?" Jackie said. "Really? Who thought of that name?"

It sounded like a character in one of her books.

Jorge just looked at her.

"Sorry sweetie," he said. "I thought about Chita Rivera, but I just couldn't pull the trigger."

Jorge was thorough, Jackie had to give him that.

The blonde barmaid huffed, like she was doing Jackie a favor serving her.

Excuse the hell out of me, lady.

Jackie lighted a cigarette and glared at the woman's retreating backside.

It's a free country, right? Would the woman be surprised if she knew Jackie's real line of work?

Of course she would.

Jackie was tired, even though she made sure to sleep regularly along the way, using a black mask like the panelists on *What's My Line*.

Jackie remembered the first job Jorge Alonso proposed to her.

She had been surprised, but didn't show it.

Could she do it? Of course she could. She had killed before. Jorge Alonso was the only one who knew it.

This time, she would be paid for it.

"You're perfect for it, Jackie," he had said. "Not much bothers you, does it?"

Which was a funny thing for Jorge to say, even though he was right.

The first man Jackie killed had just walked away free from a trial held at the Pima County Courthouse downtown.

Botched evidence and he walked.

The man had killed Jackie's best friend and he smirked when he saw Jackie in the courtroom.

Given enough time, Jackie figured the man would kill another girl and then another. Maybe her.

She didn't want that to happen. She wasn't going to let it happen.

She bought a small handgun from a guy at the Tanque Verde Swap Meet. Followed her friend's killer for three nights. Every night, he left his trailer in Flowing Wells and went to a strip bar on Miracle Mile called Castaways.

Jackie parked on the other side of the street next to a Jack in the Box where she could see him going in and out.

His routine was steady. He usually stepped into an alley next to the bar to take a leak before going home.

On the third night, Jackie was waiting for him in the alley.

She shot him three times to be sure.

Twice in the chest and once in the head.

She had parked her car a couple of streets away. Jackie took her time getting back to it, gun stuck inside the waistband of her jeans.

Back then she had worked for Jorge Alonso, just doing this and that for him in his showroom.

A week after she shot the guy, Jorge had called her back into his office.

Jorge smiled at her. He had the newspaper spread in front of him.

Tapped the article. A picture of the alley and a picture of Castaways.

"A little bird tells me you got a secret, sweetie." he said.

She looked at Jorge Alonso.

She didn't say anything. He'd known how upset she'd been and how she followed the trial.

"You've been different since all this happened," he said. "Happy almost."

She nodded.

She didn't have anything to worry about with Jorge.

"My lips are sealed, sweetie," Jorge Alonso said. "In my opinion, the world's a better place without that man."

The first job Jorge sent her on was on the east side of Mesa.

A guy skimming money from a laundromat which served as a drop for dope money. That was all he told her and that was more than he needed to tell her.

"You're an out-of-town coed, sweetie," Jorge said to her. "Think *Flashdance*. He's going to think you're there to wash your leggings."

Jorge gave Jackie instructions like she was going to her first high school dance.

"Don't look at anything, don't touch anything, get in, get out. He's the guy working behind the counter sells the little boxes of Tide. Gets you quarters if you need them. Nice guy? Unh-uh. No way, Jose. That's just what he wants you to think, like he's some poor innocent schlub."

Jackie nodded. Listening to Jorge Alonso.

"This dumbo you're going to find is very typical," Jorge said. He always called the men dumbos. "He won't know who you are and if you're as smart as I think you are, you won't know anything about him. Believe me though, Jackie. You will be doing a service to humanity."

Jackie did what she was contracted to do.

The money was good.

Afterwards, Jorge gave her more business. Jobs now out of town. Mostly up around Phoenix.

In between the jobs, Jackie rested. She lounged around the pool at the condo. Applying suntan oil and reading thick novels about glamorous people in places like Miami and Palm Springs.

In a way, Jorge was right about Jackie's emotional makeup.

Jackie never got flustered during a job. Because Jorge never gave Jackie any background information about the men she was going to target, Jackie stayed detached.

They were just dumbos to Jorge and to Jackie too.

"Look," Jorge had said. "There's a whole system of justice in this country, right?

Jackie nodded.

"That's the justice system everybody sees. It's complicated and sometimes people get away with things they shouldn't ought to, if you follow me. You and I know it has nothing to do with what's right or wrong. These dumbos? They aren't sweet and innocent, believe me. Each one has been rotten for years. Otherwise you would never come in contact with them. Jackie's performing a service, right? You don't do it, somebody else is gonna, and you can't complain about the money, sweetie, that's one thing you can't do."

The men were faceless and interchangeable as far as Jackie was concerned.

Dumbos.

Maybe her feelings would have been different if the jobs took her anywhere near the men's homes, offices or families.

She had feelings like anyone else, but refused to let her mind stray into tender areas.

These were not nice people she was dealing with.

"They're bottom feeders, baby," Jorge said. "The lowest of the low."

The sun had set before Jackie got to Albuquerque.

The waitress put the drink in front of Jackie, placing it on a turquoise cocktail napkin.

"See the man in the corner?" the waitress said.

She rolled her eyes. "He wants to know if he can buy you one."

Jackie put down the Jacqueline Susann novel. She had bought the book at a gas station after leaving Tucson.

The man wore a blue checked jacket over a white ribbed turtleneck shirt. Tan with dark hair. A whiskey drink parked in front of him. He looked like a mod Dean Martin. Not bad looking for an older guy. Jackie caught the eye and she nodded.

The man raised his eyebrows and moved his head slightly. A very smooth practiced moved.

Jackie left the novel and the drink on her table and walked over to the man.

"Anything you need to know?" he said.

Jackie shook her head no.

Jorge Alonso had given her the details.

All this guy needed to provide was the bread.

The man nodded. He looked relieved.

"You were recommended," he said. "No fuss, no muss."

Jackie nodded. She didn't need to hear her reviews. She was efficient and professional.

"After this, maybe..." the man said.

She cut him off.

"There is no *after this*," she said. "I'm just waiting for the cash. I'll go to a private place and if it's right, I'll take care of things. If the money is *not* right, I need to find out why. You don't want that situation."

"It's right," the man said. "No need to worry about it. It's right. I checked. My wife says I'm fussy about that, you know? I gotta check the door twice, make sure it's locked before we go out. Tell you what. Go get your drink and that book. I'll be leaving here in a few minutes. We'll just sit here for a little while. Have a drink together. No harm in that, is there? There's a case under this table. That's the money. Don't look now, it's all there. Twenties and hundreds. They spend easy. Take the bag when you feel comfortable. You sure you got all the details?"

"Of course," Jackie said.

She got her book. Put the drink down on the dark table.

They were two people sitting in a dark bar.

She looked maybe a little flashier than Jorge Alonso would have liked, but Jorge wasn't here.

Besides, she wouldn't look like this when she did the job.

Right now there was nothing unusual going on in this Ramada Inn. Nothing out of the ordinary.

"What's the book?" the man said.

He leaned forward. They had some time to kill making things look right.

"It's nothing," Jackie said. "Just something I picked up."

"I'm not kidding. I'm curious. My wife is a reader. You wouldn't believe how much she reads. If it's something good, maybe I'll get it for her. Like, if it's sexy, that's what I'm talking about. She likes books like that. She gets romantic. If it's got a lot of action, she gets really romantic."

"Nice for you," Jackie said.

He was an okay guy. She was glad he wasn't the guy she would kill.

"Exactly," he said. "Nice for me. Bada bing."

"Rimshot," Jackie said.

"So seriously, what's the book?"

She turned the book over showed him the cover with the statuette and the eyes.

"It's called *Once is Not Enough*," she said.

"Sounds promising," the guy said. "Is it sexy?"

"It's okay," she said. "Nothing to write home about."

She pushed the book toward the man.

"Take it. I've read enough of it. Give it to your wife. See what happens."

Jackie winked at him.

❊ ❊ ❊

After getting the bag from the guy in the bar, Jackie did a quick look at the money. She changed from the corporate outfit into a mini-skirt and platinum wig.

Near the guy's shop, Jackie stepped out of the electric blue rental Impala.

All Jackie had to do was complete the job.

She took the Savage out from her purse and pulled the slide, making sure there was a round in the chamber.

She got out of her car and started walking toward the shop. The dress shoes she wore weren't good on the cinders of the shop driveway, but Jackie figured they lent authenticity.

Jorge had given Jackie the second man's description. He was going to be at his shop.

There were two lifts in the place and a Dodge Aspen in the drive.

Signed pictures of Richard Boone and Connie Stevens over the cash register along with a framed dollar bill.

The guy was surprised when he saw Jackie coming into the shop, but he was all smiles. She looked good and maybe he figured he would be getting lucky tonight.

He had that kind of look on his face, anyway. Who could say exactly what he was thinking?

Who could say how he figured he could get away cleanly with cheating on his partners? Jackie didn't have to worry about getting back the money he'd stolen and she wasn't there to psychoanalyze him. That wasn't part of the job.

She had one job tonight.

He was maybe fifty years old. Fleshy around the neck.

"Hey mister," she said. "My car broke down. Can you help me?"

He looked around. Just finishing up for the night.

"Where is it?" he said.

He didn't ask anything else. He started to get up. He wasn't dressed for mechanical work. He had on a coral leisure suit with a spread shirt collar.

"It's a little ways from here," she said. "I walked for a little bit."

"What's wrong with it?" he said.

"I don't know anything about cars," Jackie said. "It just made a funny noise and then conked out. I don't have much money with me but I can pay you back."

"Funny noise," he said. "Just gimme a second to lock this place up. I was leaving."

The Dodge smelled like Aqua Velva.

By the time he got behind the drivers wheel, Jackie had the Savage leveled at him. She was three feet from his open driver's side window.

She didn't like the smirk he gave her when she told him to hand over his wallet.

The guy just figured this was a cheap stickup.

He wouldn't have time to learn otherwise.

She didn't take it personally. Jackie didn't take things personally when she was working.

The wallet thing was just something she did. For one thing, it took the guy's eyes away from her. She didn't want the wallet. She never kept anything from the job except the fee.

"What do you got in mind, baby?" he said.

Funny last words.

What do you got in mind?

He dropped his head before she shot him.

She didn't need ten shots.

Just three shots quick.

*   *   *

Jackie Fuller, looking older now in blue jeans and a sweatshirt was on a street three blocks from the courthouse in Holbrook, Arizona.

She was steps away from the petrified wood shop and the railroad tracks. The car wouldn't last long here on the street.

She had covered a lot of miles from the Dodge Aspen in Albuquerque. She had covered her tracks.

The sun had not come up yet.

Enormous concrete dinosaurs stood in front of the white adobe shop, inviting tourists to stop and take pictures.

The truck driver who picked Jackie up wanted to stop at Earl's Restaurant in Gallup and could use some company. After getting fuel he said he would drive her on I-40 all the way to Holbrook. The truck driver was going to be turning north in Holbrook, delivering concrete to Kayenta on the Navajo Nation.

At Holbrook, Jackie would head south.

She had gotten the ride with the truck driver about two hours before. Earl's Restaurant had just opened for the day and the driver bought her breakfast.

She hated riding buses. She could have bought a used car anywhere on the road for cash, but that was a hassle.

Jackie had money and a driver's license.

The driver's license Jackie carried was from Florida and was a fake. It didn't have the same name Jorge had put on the diner card. This one said Carol Brady.

Jackie groaned.

The money the first guy gave her was banded and lay flat on the bottom of her backpack.

"You want to head up there with me?" the driver said. He wasn't a bad guy. Jackie liked him. He had learned diesel mechanics at Fort Leonard Wood while serving in the Army and he hadn't made a big deal out of giving Jackie a ride. He could fix these rigs, but he didn't want to be penned into a mechanic job. Too much like being stuck in a cage. He liked being out on the road seeing the country.

He hadn't made any moves toward her, just grinned a little and asked her a few questions, but not too many, about her trip.

They were almost to the turnoff in Holbrook. He would turn north and head to Kayenta and she would get out and pick up another ride to get back to Tucson. At the intersection there were already two men with their thumbs out.

The driver looked at Jackie.

"Interesting country up there if you've never seen it before."

Jackie looked at him.

She thought about what she had waiting for her in Tucson.

Jorge Alonso and his mimosas. Jackie could send him his cut and she would be done.

Jackie smiled at the truck driver.

"Sounds like fun," she said.

THE KATSINA

Billy Valentine, opening his eyes, glanced at the Smith and Wesson Model 10.

No fancy guns for Billy Valentine.

The gun was the last thing he put away at night, and consequently, the first thing he saw when he woke up in the morning. He kept the loaded revolver on the table next to the bed in the place most people keep their alarm clock. You don't always need an alarm clock but you never can tell when you might need a gun, and Valentine's Model 10 was reliable.

Billy Valentine's eyes always opened when he needed to wake up. Today he had to get up early.

This morning, six o'clock felt much too early.

Valentine got out of bed, put on blue jeans, went into the kitchen to make coffee. Stood around waiting until there was enough to half-fill a mug.

The same old morning ritual. This morning just earlier than usual.

Valentine would head down from the Mogollon Rim through the Salt River Canyon toward Tucson. The trip would take four hours if

Valentine didn't push it. Just in time to get to the art auction at the Western Way

Valentine ran a horsehair brush across his boots, pulled the Navajo silver bola tie over his head and under the collar of a blue oxford cloth shirt. Slung the concha belt over his jeans.

The concha was second phase Dine'. The work of a craftsman maybe a hundred years ago.

Rare, valuable, the conchas themselves hammered from silver dollars.

The sun was barely creeping up the the mountain this time of the morning. The woods around Billy Valentine's house were still dark.

Yesterday, Valentine heard shots from the other side of the barbed wire fence separating National Forest from reservation land.

It was elk season on the rez, but there were too many shots to be a hunter. The thing sounded like a cannon, though.

Somebody was out there doing something. Probably shooting at the refrigerator somebody had dumped illegally a few months before. The shooting was none of Billy Valentine's concern.

He could tell the weather would be cold today.

Winter was coming but there was still time to appreciate the fall.

Valentine wouldn't say he loved winter's approach, but he appreciated the change of seasons the same way he appreciated a piece of art, a symphony, or a beautiful woman.

When he went to the city, Valentine never left the mountain completely behind.

Valentine took his gray Resistol from the hook next to the front door. Looked out the door at the sky.

The Mogollon Rim was most beautiful at this time of the year.

Valentine's cabin was hidden deep among the ponderosa pines, backed by land owned by the tribe. The cabin was big enough for Valentine, but not elaborate. Not fussy like some of the places at the country club. Valentine had bought the cabin from a Phoenix doctor. Valentine never met the doctor but he had been told the guy built the place for his retirement before discovering his breathing became sluggish at seven thousand feet.

The doctor hadn't counted on the high elevation of the Mogollon Rim kicking his ass.

At seven thousand feet above sea level you couldn't expect to do everything the way you did in the valley. People had to adjust or they couldn't stay on the mountain.

Valentine took his coffee and stood next to the stone fireplace. The embers were gone from last night's fire leaving only a powdery white ash. Valentine stirred what was left making sure. Nothing. The fire was dead.

Something out the window caught Valentine's eye. He turned and looked.

On the edge of the forest, four elk stood near the ponderosa pine.

The elk were sentinels, guarding the perimeter of the woods.

It was rare seeing them this close to town.

Sensing Valentine's attention, they bolted into the forest.

They were reservation elk now.

The coffee at the bottom of the mug was cold. Valentine threw the dregs into the ashes.

Valentine looked at the stack of alligator juniper next to the fireplace. The gnarly logs burned better than any other wood cut on the mountain.

Valentine bought the wood on the border of the White Mountain Apache reservation. Rodney Armstrong made the delivery in his beat-up Ford pickup, dumping the cord and a half on the needles next to the cabin. Valentine still had logs to split before the weather got much colder.

Valentine had seen several elk in the last couple of days. He'd seen a couple last night on the way home from Eddie C's.

He had come *this* close to hitting one of them with his truck.

Elk grazed along the length of the Mogollon Rim. You had to be careful at night. Stay alert behind the wheel. Valentine only barely had enough time to avoid hitting the massive creature.

It had been late.

Damn poker game was pointless.

Playing a George Strait tape in the truck, thinking about the steak dinner, but mostly thinking about Theresa at Eddie C's. The steak was substantial and he thought Theresa had been extra friendly.

Valentine couldn't say how big the elk was, it got away too quickly. Big enough, though. The rack of antlers on the buck would have destroyed his truck and could have killed Valentine

* * *

Junior Gates worked the morning shift at the Triangle Market. He had worked at the convenience store for exactly one month and a day.

He had begun to feel comfortable in the place, not craning his neck to look over his shoulder all the time now. The boss had enough confidence in Junior to leave him on his own and now Junior was opening the place. Junior liked the kind of trust the boss was showing him now.

The boss didn't treat Junior as if he was a kid or like somebody he pitied.

Junior liked working there.

He'd always liked the Triangle Market.

Junior had walked to the Triangle Market back when he was a kid, practicing his cross-over dribble in the cinders, buying a Fudgsicle if he had the money, scuffing his PF Flyers under the solitary hoop in the dusty parking lot until the sun went down.

Junior wasn't a kid any more. He was six foot

five in his stocking feet and he was twenty-three years old. He was trying to do something with his life.

Junior went to the Triangle Market Monday through Saturday to work.

He came in just after sunrise. Junior liked seeing the sunrise after a good night's sleep instead of at the tail end of an all-night party.

It felt better this way.

For a while, some of Junior's old friends had come into the Triangle Market while he was working. They laughed and joked around, maybe buying a pack of smokes, grabbing an orange Nehi out of the coke machine.

Dang, it came with the territory. The guys didn't want to see Junior make something of himself.

All they could see was him sweeping out the place and that made Junior look like a loser to them.

Junior didn't care.

They stopped coming after the first week when they figured out Junior wasn't going to party with them anymore. He wasn't going to party with them or anybody else.

Junior felt good for the first time in a while. Maybe as long as he could remember.

Junior hadn't had a drink or a drug in four months and one day.

At ninety days, the boss gave him the job at the Triangle Market.

Four months sober. One month on the job.

Both were records for Junior.

He stayed sober through the Fourth of July and also Labor Day, which was saying something. Those were big days on the rez.

Not taking a drink was his biggest accomplishment in life so far and now he was beginning to let himself think about the future, something he hadn't done since he was a little kid shooting hoops, dreaming about his basketball future.

The hoop dreams hadn't just been fantasy. Junior could have been something. With his size and his moves people talked about him.

Apache Thunder they called him in the Arizona Republic.

Junior had thrown everything away when he started drinking. Not just basketball. Everything.

His new friends, the ones helping Junior stay sober, told him not to worry about that.

All that was in the past, and there was nothing Junior could do to change it.

Focus on what you're doing now.

What Junior was doing now was sweeping the Triangle Market out and getting the place ready before the first customers came in.

It was early. Nobody had come in yet and probably wouldn't for a while. Junior put on the coffee. Decaf with the orange rim, full-strength with green.

Junior wanted to make the place look good. He wanted to take pride in what he did.

He couldn't help wondering if maybe he could still play ball but he didn't want to fool himself about hoops.

Maybe he could start at a community college. People had never seen moves like Junior made.

Not from a guy the size of Junior.

Like a Native Pistol Pete.

No-look passes over his shoulder. Pulling up for impossible jump shots way downtown.

Junior was sweeping now. Making the Triangle Market look good.

Doing what he could do today.

Junior was busy.

He didn't see the guy who was getting out of his car outside the Triangle Market.

He didn't see the guy take the gun out of the car and pull the balaclava down over his head.

* * *

Nicky Fall got out of the beige Jeep and rolled the balaclava down over his face before going into the Triangle Market.

The tourist map was still next to the steering wheel. It wasn't much of a map. Cartoon drawings of people with goofy looks on their faces pulling trout from streams like there was nothing to it.

The map had shown him the way to this place. The Triangle Market. Kind of a trading post. The place looked perfect.

Nicky Fall had driven down with the gun and his mask under his seat. Powerbait and fishhooks were next to him. Fishing pole in the back. He looked like any out of towner in search of mountain fun.

* * *

The sun would be up soon. Valentine needed to get on the road.

Valentine glanced at his empty cup and walked to the kitchen for more coffee.

The doctor had built an enormous pantry in back of the kitchen. Enough for a year's worth of food, probably.

On a sliding shelf in the back, Valentine had installed a gun safe from Western Drug.

Standing in front of the safe, Valentine punched the combination.

Valentine took out the katsina carving from the safe.

An exquisite piece.

Valentine had acquired the katsina near Shungopavi.

The center of the Hopi universe.

He unfolded a piece of black velvet and stood the katsina on the cloth. A mudhead, with a blank expression, one leg raised at the knee.

He'd paid a lot on Second Mesa for the katsina. He was going to take the carving to the auction. The katsina was listed with a photograph in the catalog, so Valentine was obligated to take it down to Tucson, but he didn't really want to let it go. He knew the value of the katsina, and had given fair payment for it. Valentine wouldn't compromise the reputation he enjoyed as a trader by cheating.

If the katsina didn't meet the reserve, Valentine would bring it back and be happy to do so. He particularly liked this katsina.

He put the bills he needed in his wallet. Valentine didn't like the idea of walking around without cash. Unexpected expenses always arose going to the city.

Valentine took two bands of bills from the safe and put them to the side. There were paintings he wanted to see. If he wanted to bid on any of them, he would need cash. Valentine didn't use banks.

He folded the velvet around the katsina and put it, with the bills, into his leather overnight bag.

Valentine hesitated, then reached into the safe for another box of cartridges.

* * *

Officer Kenny Kasey and Officer Edmund Waters were almost there. Kasey, seated behind the wheel of the Crown Victoria, Waters cupping his hand outside the patrol car's open window.

The neighborhood called *Country Living* was on their right. Kasey wouldn't have minded letting the younger man drive right now. He wouldn't have minded Waters driving all day, but before the day was over he knew they would each take a turn. The Apache reservation covered a lot of territory, from the ski area to the Salt River Canyon. Kasey and Waters never knew where the day would take them.

Kasey slowed the car down at the white-framed Missionary Lutheran church at the beginning of town, made a right hand turn, and parked the car near the supermarket.

The men climbed out of the squad car and checked out the Bashas' parking lot. Food vendors with their tailgates down. T-shirts and hand-crafted dream catchers. The men were met by the smell of fry bread cooking in oil over juniper wood fire.

Kasey bought stew in a cardboard bowl with foil stretched over.

"Health food, right?" Waters said. He had gone into Bashas' and worked his way through the store all the way back to the dairy where he had picked out a carton of boysenberry yogurt. Waters peeled off the top of the paper cup and stirred the fruit up from the bottom.

"It tastes pretty good, then," Kasey said.

He took another bite of the stew. The meat

was very lean. Tough but flavorful.

"I know you want some of this."

He pointed with his chin toward the bowl.

"Not now," Waters said. "Gotta give my stomach a break. You go ahead."

"Community center, right?" Waters said. "See what's new up there?"

Kasey folded a tortilla and scraped the last of the stew from the bowl. Tossed the bowl, spoon, and foil in an overflowing container.

A black and brown dog looked up at Kasey.

"Sorry, champ," Kasey said. "All gone."

He pointed at Edmund Waters.

"Try him," Kasey said. "He's got a big heart."

"Let's go," Waters said.

The community center was surrounded by cottonwood trees and was a brown cinder block building standing in the center of the village.

At the community center, the two men dropped a case of Folgers coffee, red and green in the dusty kitchen where Loreena Gray made a fuss over the two men.

"Here you go, Mrs. Olson," Kasey said to Loreena.

Loreena Gray was an elected official from Greenlake. She was wearing her traditional camp dress, beaded earrings and a beaded American flag brooch for the meeting.

Loreena smiled when the two officers placed the cans of coffee on the kitchen counter.

"Meeting starts right after noon," she said.

"You staying?"

"Wish we could," Waters said. "Got to go check on some things. Maybe come back later."

The meetings could go on well into the early evening until everyone had their say.

"You boys going out to catch bad guys?" Loreena said.

The officers exchanged glances.

"Something going on, Loreena? Something I should know about?" Waters said.

Kasey nodded in the direction of the Bunn coffee maker on the counter. A stack of Styrofoam cups and an open box of Domino sugar cubes next to the machine.

"That ready, Loreena?"

"Take a cup and see, then," Loreena said. She swatted at Kasey as he walked next to her, catching his forearm with a Manila folder. "Be my guest. You boys are doing a good job, though."

"We keep busy, anyway," Kasey said.

Waters laughed. "Alias Smith and Jones, they call us. Native Edition."

Loreena smiled at the men.

"How's the coffee?" she said.

Kasey pulled one of the cups off the stack. There was something damp around the top of the cup, and when he tasted the coffee, it tasted like the cups had been stored too close to the sugar.

"It tastes real good, Loreena. It's just like I like it. Can't beat rez coffee, can you?"

Waters was looking at the Xeroxed notices

tacked to the bulletin board when Kasey came out of the community center.

"Dance this weekend, up at Seven Mile. You going?"

"Hell no," Kasey said. "Can't do it. Not anymore. I got too much respect for my back now. I get a day off, I rest up."

He put his hand on his lower back, just above his service weapon.

"I'm not getting any younger, either."

They pulled the car to the side of the road, just after the turnoff.

It would not be a busy day. This was fall. Hunting season. You could feel the chill in the air.

Kasey pushed the lighter into the dash.

"You think the council is going to go for that casino?" Waters said.

This was an old subject and Waters worked it like a hungry dog.

Kasey waited.

"Maybe. It could bring in money, if we get one," he said.

"Yeah, but for who? Who gets that money?"

"Thought that one guy was gonna. The white guy came up here."

"Waterman was going to make money," Waters said.

Kasey shook his head.

"Guess he won't now," he said. "Hear anything more about that?"

"Nothing to hear," Waters said. "Man jumped

out the window of his office eight floors up."

"Doesn't matter," Kasey said. "Those guys can smell money. Give it some time, you're just gonna get another Waterman."

"What nobody says is who's gonna go to the place off-season, right?" Waters said. "What about when the white guys aren't around? Who's gonna sit in front of the slots then?"

"People who got no money," Kasey said.

He took a sip of the coffee from the Styrofoam lidded cup.

"Every dollar you make from a white guy, you're going to get three or four from people can't afford it."

Kasey was tired of the subject. Tired of going through it with Waters. Things were always going to change, weren't they? Things always changed. You want to stay the same, you're out of luck. Even on the reservation.

Kasey lighted a cigarette and took another sip of the coffee.

Waters looked at him.

"Gimme one, I'm out."

Kasey laughed.

"You're always out. I'll stop at Triangle Market you can get some of your own. Buy me a pack, too.

He shook a cigarette out and handed the pack to Waters.

"I'll get some more coffee, too," Kasey said. "Still gonna be a long day. Should have filled my thermos."

He hadn't been bullshitting Loreena.

There really wasn't anything like rez coffee.

Not on a chilly early morning like this one.

* * *

A cowbell rang on the inside handle when Nicky pushed the door open.

Nicky looked at the stack of Blue Bird Flour bags and the empty store.

He must be the first customer of the day. A really good situation.

The store clerk saw Nicky holding the gun.

He was a big Indian. Tall. Lanky.

Looked like he was in shape, not that it mattered.

He was holding a broom and wore an apron.

"Don't shoot," the store clerk said. "Take what you want, bro. Be my guest."

That was *exactly* what he said. His exact words.

Be my guest.

Which would have made Nicky laugh usually, a big dude like this one with the ponytail.

This dude looked *scared.*

Why wouldn't he be frightened?

Fear was what Nicky wanted. Fear and compliance. That's why Nicky bought the Colt. It was fierce-looking, and anyone could see what it would do.

You hit a man with this thing, hell, don't matter where, guarantee you he's going down.

The man at the pawnshop in Holbrook sold the weapon to Nicky for cash.

No questions asked.

New management, the sign had said.

He'd gotten a shoulder holster too. Practiced pulling the weapon in the mirror at his motel room.

Like Travis Bickle in *Taxi Driver*.

You talkin' to me?

The Colt worked, man. Nicky had run some rounds through it last night out on the rez. Seeing what was what. Shot into an abandoned refrigerator then picked up the shell casings before he left. No reason to leave a track for the fuzz.

Be my guest.

Now wasn't the time for Nicky to laugh.

"Cool, bro," Nicky said. "I just gotta put these on you."

Keeping things cordial while bringing the zip-ties and duct tape out of his bag, motioning the big guy to turn around. Trying to make it sound like Nicky was just doing a job. Cool, relaxed, impersonal.

"Under the tray," the guy said. Nicky scooped up the ones, fives and tens out of the cash register. Next to nothing in here.

He almost grabbed the change, then left it.

He pulled up on the zip ties and taped the guy's wrists and ankles. Houdini might have been able to get out of the rig Nicky set up, but this big dude wouldn't be going anywhere for a while.

Sure enough, three twenties lay under the tray, just like the Tooth Fairy left them.

Nicky looked behind the counter and grabbed three cartons of Marlboro cigarettes.

The tape would keep the big Indian busy. He could try to bite his way through, but the guy was probably too big to be able to bend down and work on the tape.

Nicky pulled the balaclava off as soon as he walked out the door of the convenience store. The damn thing was itchy as hell. He rubbed the top of his nose between his eyes. The wool was scratchy, like maybe he was allergic to it or something. He shoulda gotten something else like maybe a Halloween mask. Something easy on and easy off. You live and you learn. The balaclava was overkill. Some people would say the gun and the robbery itself was overkill, but Nicky didn't give a shit what other people said.

Nicky Fall wasn't really used to even being awake at this hour. He was starting to get hungry. He could have grabbed a couple Slim Jims on his way out, but it would be dumb to go back in.

He'd done pretty well and it was time to get moving.

The money wasn't even the damn point, was it? This was practice. Seeing what kind of nerve he had. If there was more than a hundred dollars in the register Nicky would be surprised.

Still, he'd made out okay. And Nicky knew it wasn't the guy's money.

The big Indian guy was getting hourly from whoever owned the place. Maybe after this, the guy would quit. Standing behind a counter was no way to live. In a way, Nicky had done the guy a favor.

The zip-ties and duct tape were just to buy a little time. Nicky just needed a little head start. Enough time to get off the rez.

On the way out the door, Nicky grabbed a sky blue T-shirt off the rack.

Extra-large.

Nicky wore a large size but these things shrink.

Fry Bread Power.

Nicky liked that.

Power to the people.

Being tied up behind the door, the big guy didn't even see him grab the shirt. In a way, that gave Nicky even more of a feeling of accomplishment than he'd felt grabbing the money.

Nicky opened the front door of the Jeep. Tossed the cartons of smokes and the T-shirt in the passenger side of the car.

One more time congratulating himself on the paint job.

Earl Scheib had charged him thirty-nine ninety five to cover the car with beige paint. Before, the Jeep's orange paint-job screamed for attention.

The beige made the Jeep look like a rock. You pass it and you don't notice it. Like it wasn't even there. Good color for the desert.

Nicky Fall looked in the bag where he'd put the money. Because it was cold he could see his breath in the air.

The cash was dirty. Who the hell knew how many hands these bills passed through to get to this place?

There wasn't much cash. Outside of the three twenties, there were just a bunch of grubby one dollar bills.

Three twenties, a couple fives and a ten and the ones. Maybe a hundred and something total?

Time for breakfast, then.

Nicky was hungry. Usually, he just made do with instant coffee and a cig.

Today, Nicky was hungry. He wanted a real breakfast.

You can't have a revolution without breaking a few eggs, right?

The thought made him laugh.

He could get something to eat up in town

Nicky was going through the town on his way off the mountain and knew something would be open.

❋ ❋ ❋

"Need anything?" Kasey said.

Waters shook his head no.

Kasey headed into the Triangle Market. You couldn't get a whole lot there, but he liked the place. He liked the girl who sometimes was behind the counter. Triangle Market was just a little out of town.

Farther out of town than *Country Living*. He was thinking about getting the new George Strait cassette. There were some good songs on it and Kasey liked the kind of country music made you think about honky tonks. The girl he'd been thinking about wasn't behind the counter. Nobody was behind the counter. The place looked empty. Wide open and empty.

Kasey looked around. There wasn't much to the place. Fishing tackle, T-shirts, cigarettes. They were selling basketball shoes now. The King Ropes hats display was knocked over on its side and the screened back door was swinging open.

The drawer to the cash register was open and empty.

Kasey went back to the front door. Waters waiting next to the car smoking a cigarette. Kasey signaled to Waters.

Neither of the men spoke.

Kasey held his service weapon in front of him and entered the building again.

The guy was behind the door. Not the girl Kasey liked, the guy who worked here. The big guy. Kasey remembered he had played basketball. He'd been pretty good.

Kasey kept watch while Waters got the duct

tape off the guy's mouth, legs, ankles.

"What happened?" Waters said.

The big guy shook his head. Kasey remembered his name. Junior Gates.

"Junior," Kasey said, "what happened."

Junior didn't talk right away. He looked up at Kasey and Waters.

"Guy's gone. I didn't do nothing. Guy wants a hundred bucks so bad, I'm not dying for that."

"This guy," Waters said. "You recognize him?"

"He had on a mask, bro. One of those knit things, like he was in the movies," Junior was picking at the tape still on his legs. "Mask and a gun. Big handgun."

"That's it?" Waters said. "A hundred he got?"

"Yep. That's what I had for the start of the day. He took some smokes, too," Junior said.

He clutched at his leg.

"Damn. I'm stiff all over. Marlboro reds he took. Couple cartons."

Junior lifted his arm up, pushed his hands together then shook them.

"He was a white guy, though. I saw that."

"You sure he was a white guy? He had on a mask, right?"

Junior nodded.

"This guy was white as shit. Wearing moccasins though, like he was going Native."

Kasey had gone to the car to call the station.

"You need anything, Junior?" Waters said. He

was standing next to the cooler.

Junior was on the floor, his legs stretched in front of him. Still shaking his head.

"Get me a Dr Pepper bro. You want one too, take it. Don't make no difference. Boss won't mind."

Waters uncapped a bottle and handed it to Junior.

"Anything else?"

Junior took a swig.

"Nope. I'm calling my boss and heading home."

Kasey came back in.

"Gonna have to stay here for a while," he said. "Where's the phone?"

"Over there," Junior toward the cash register. "Right by the calenders."

"Maybe you call him. Tell him what happened. You want I can talk."

"Ain't nothing," Junior said. "I'll call."

Kasey turned to Waters.

"Gonna be a long day," he said. "Get comfortable. Gotta write out a statement, wait for the detective. Since it's a white guy, probably gotta contact the feds."

Waters opened the front door, paused, then flipped around the cardboard sign from open to closed.

He turned back to Kasey.

"I'll put up some yellow tape," he said. "No need for looky-loos."

* * *

Billy Valentine drove his pickup onto Arizona State Route 260. He would stop for breakfast at Casa Molina, a small adobe restaurant ringed by cedar and aspen trees.

He took his rifle from the rack in the cab and locked it in his tool case. He carried the rifle in the cab everywhere he went on the mountain, but he was headed to Tucson.

No sense keeping it in the gun rack where it could get stolen.

He had put his holstered Smith and Wesson in a sling he'd rigged under the dashboard. The leather bag holding his money and the katsina was on the seat next to him.

The weather was good. A day like this made you optimistic. There would be snow before long. During winter, unpredictable snow on the Mogollon Rim would make some of these roads impassible. For now it was a beautiful day with a high blue sky over the ponderosa pines.

The only other car in the parking lot was Gus's white Monte Carlo.

Opposite the counter, Gus had a fire going in the black iron stove. The stovepipe went straight up through the low ceiling of the restaurant. The fire made Casa Molina cozy.

The place smelled good.

Valentine grabbed a menu from the counter

although he didn't need one. Gus and Evelyn Molina offered a choice between a red or a green chili. Their specials were numbered one through seven.

No substitutions unless you asked really nice.

Gus Molina set black coffee in front of Valentine. The smell of the strong coffee competed with freshly roasted Hatch chile peppers.

Gus wore a Blue Ridge Yellow Jackets sweatshirt. He mopped the red and white oilcloth tablecloth with a rag before setting the coffee down. Gus was skinny and the sweatshirt was too big for him. His son Miguel played for the Yellow Jackets.

"You're dressing fancy today, Billy," Gus said. "What you got going on?"

"I'm going down to the big city, Gus," Valentine said. "Might be gone a few days. Keep things nice till I get back, right?"

"Hollywood? They finally call you?"

"Tucson, Gus."

Gus laughed. "I thought you said *big* city."

"Semi-big, Gus."

"You going to be back for the game Friday?" Gus said. "Snowflake." He shook his head. "It's going to be a tough one. Them boys are *always* big. This year they're quick."

Valentine lifted the cup of coffee and cocked his head.

"Hope I can make it. I should be back by

137

then."

"You must be working, dressed like that?"

Valentine sipped the coffee, looked at the paper mat in front of him advertising plumbers and accountants on the moutain. There was a word search puzzle and Valentine spotted 'cholla.'

He put the cup down. Drummed his fingers on the counter.

Gus smiled, shook his head. Billy Valentine never talked about his work.

"Get a tag this year?" Valentine said. He thought for a second about the elk in his backyard this morning. Then he thought about the gunfire he heard.

"I put in," Gus said. "So did Miggy. So did Evelyn. We'll see what happens."

"Why not get one of your buddies on the rez get you a tag, Gus?"

"Yeah right," Gus said. "Maybe I'll do that. You know what they charge for one of those? They save those for big-shots, right? George Strait and them. They fly those guys in, I'll guarantee you they're gonna get their elk."

Valentine laughed. "You could be the middle-man or something. Maybe cook for 'em."

"You shoulda seen this guy just left." Gus said, "I'd swear he was who, Charles Bronson? I get Evelyn out of the kitchen, she comes out, the guy's sitting back there in that booth back there. Looks just like him except what he's wearing." Gus pointed at the booth farthest from the door.

"Sitting right there. I point him out to Evelyn, real quiet. *Death Wish*, right? He'd ordered green chili, this one, he knows what he's doing. Has his chili in front of him, got his tortillas just like he's a *vato*. Coulda swore he was Charles Bronson. Looked just like him."

"You talk to him?" Valentine said.

"Naah," Gus said. "It wasn't him, Billy. I seen Bronson enough in movies, I oughta know what he looks like. This guy here, he looks more just like he's a regular guy. This guy's just sitting there, got on a T-shirt says something about fry bread. Man, he looks just like Bronson though. I even got Evelyn to go back in the kitchen get the Polaroid camera just in case it's him."

Gus pointed at the hall leading to the men's and lady's rooms. There were probably a hundred fading pictures of people sitting behind scoops of fried ice cream Gus and Evelyn served on customer's birthdays. All of them wearing the green velvet sombrero hung in the hallway.

"She take his picture?"

"Evelyn asked him."

"What'd he say?"

"You kidding? Whattya think he's gonna say? 'No way,' he says," Gus said. He smiled. "He looked at me like I was a cop. I backed up then, cause he didn't look like such a good guy, then. So whatta we know? I just tell Evelyn, 'put away the camera, Evelyn'. That's what I said to her kinda quiet. He was giving Evelyn a bad feeling too,

Billy. Brought him some extra butter tortillas, you know? I'm thinking maybe I've got him wrong. Maybe he's just held up an armored car. Like one of those movies, right? He's waiting for the rest of the team. Like he's in the middle of a heist. He's waiting for his money, right? Crazy as hell, you can bet on that. Like we get crosswise he could just go ahead and shoot us because he thinks we're gonna call the fuzz."

Valentine laughed.

"All this you're thinking while the guy's sitting there eating his chili?

Gus nodded.

"Sure, Billy. You shoulda seen the look the guy gave me. You never know who you get around here. All kinds of people," Gus said.

"I'll bet," Valentine said.

"Then I start to think. Where'd his other people go, anyway? The ones on his team. Nobody does a job like that alone. Like what, they double-cross him?"

Valentine lighted a cigarette. Enjoying himself. Gus Molina could tell a hell of a story, even if the whole thing had only gone on in his head.

"That's what your guy's wondering, Gus. He's just done some kind of job, he can't be too sure what he's going to do next. Maybe he's got the money, but not all of it. He's going around like a wounded animal. A coyote or something. He figures they got the other guys in custody and just aren't releasing that on the news. If that's the case, he knows he's screwed. Maybe the cops were here before him. He doesn't know. If the cops *were* there, he figures they musta told you about him. Told you to get his picture, right? Take his picture with the Polaroid. If it's a two man job, our guy's the big winner if the other guy's dead. If they caught the other guy, he's gotta run. But here you and Evelyn come with your Polaroid camera, right? The guy's gonna be a little edgy, right?"

Gus looked at Valentine. Not saying anything, just listening.

"If your guy has the money, all he's got to do is lay low, right?" Valentine said. "Winter comes, he's got it made. Maybe he slides down past Hannigan Meadow, down past Morenci and all that. You've been hunting there, haven't you, Gus? Nobody on that road. He makes it through there, he's got a clear shot to Mexico."

Gus Molina shook his head.

"You figure the guy would do it that way, Billy?"

"That's the way I'd do it, I guess. Not that I've thought about it much."

"So, he comes in here and I turn him in, they're gonna kiss my ass and put my picture in the paper, right?"

"Pretty much, Gus. You'd be the only thing between him and Mexico. If you live, you end up a hero."

The chili came with homemade tortillas.

Evelyn brought the plate out, steaming from

the kitchen.

Valentine stubbed out his cigarette in the little tin Casa Molina ashtray next to the napkin dispenser.

Valentine ate the chili. It really was the best on the mountain.

"How much you think a guy like that would have with him?" Gus said.

Valentine laughed.

"Some guy comes in here like that?" Valentine said, "you're gonna do the right thing, Gus, aren't you?"

Gus nodded his head.

"Sure Billy," he said. "I get on the phone and call you, right?"

Valentine laughed.

"You got that right, Gus. You get on the damn phone and call me. We'll split whatever they got."

"Sound's like a plan, Billy.

Valentine got up and looked out the window.

"All I know is, that guy left in a hurry," Gus said. "Paid up and left. I stood right where you were and watched him peel out."

"What was he driving, Gus?"

Valentine paid for his breakfast and Gus brought him a lidded Styrofoam cup with coffee.

"Jeep," Gus said. "Looked kinda tan, I guess."

Valentine stood in front of the glass counter. Under the glass there were pictures of Gus and his family standing in front of the white Monte Carlo.

Gus's pride and joy. Dayton wire rims and a landau roof.

Another picture of Gus and Miguel, kneeling with rifles in front of an elk.

"You still selling those cards for the booster club?"

Gus nodded. "Still got two or three, I guess."

"I'll take a couple."

Gus leaned under the counter and brought out a couple of the cards and Valentine paid for them.

"All kinds of good stuff on those, Billy," Gus said. "Helps the team, too."

Valentine nodded. "Happy to do it, Gus. Tell Miggy good luck in the playoffs, right?"

"I'll do that. Maybe see you next game. Snowflake, right?"

"I'll take a paper, too."

Gus handed Valentine the paper. Nothing interesting on the front page. Stuff about the fire season which was over for the year. Valentine washed his hands before leaving Gus's restaurant, holding the paper cup of coffee while pulling down a length of the cloth towel dispenser.

In the parking lot, Valentine looked down at his boots and the red dust from the cinder parking lot.

He would get them shined later at the Western Way.

Valentine got in his pickup.

Winter was coming. Maybe he'd go down to

Rocky Point for a while and do some fishing.

He pulled out of the parking lot of the Hacienda Molina, turning left again on State Route 260. His rifle in the back was loaded and so was the Smith, holstered under the dash.

He would drive through Show Low, then through the Salt River Canyon on U.S. Highway 60.

* * *

Show Low, Arizona.

Named by the turn of a card.

By the time Valentine reached the town, the elevation had dropped.

Turning left on the Deuce of Clubs he drove from Show Low on U.S. Route 60.

Valentine passed the small pine tree covered year-round with Christmas ornaments. Passed a campaign sign from the tribal election. Painted blue with yellow lettering, the plywood sign was held in place by T-bars driven into the caliche.

Valentine drove south toward the start of the Salt River Canyon. The trees were changing from the aspen and pine to scrub cedar. The altitude was lower. Valentine looked at his watch. It was later than he thought.

He hit the accelerator.

Valentine unscrewed the lid from the coffee. There was still some warmth in the cup.

He punched the cigarette lighter into the dash, waited until it popped out, holding the coffee in one hand with the steering wheel, lighting a Camel with the other.

❋ ❋ ❋

Billy Valentine knew these two. He knew all the sheriff's deputies, the local cops, the tribal guys. He knew Kenny Kasey and Edmund Waters.

Barriers had been erected on the reservation line. Kasey and Waters were checking cars and trucks individually.

Passing through was going to be a no-go.

"What's going on?" Valentine said.

Edmund Waters was younger than Kasey. He had on big aviators and wore his hair a little longer than his partner.

Waters smiled seeing Valentine.

"Stopping people, seeing who's coming this way. There was a holdup down outside town."

"Holdup?" Valentine said.

"Guy pulled a gun at the Triangle Market." Waters said. "Clerk says it was a white guy."

Valentine nodded.

"That's your description? A white guy?"

"He had a mask on," Waters said. "One of those wool caps you pull down so they cover their face."

"Right," Valentine said. "I'll keep my eyes open."

Kasey laughed.

"Pretty sure he got that mask off by now,"

"We're stopping everybody," Waters said. "Can't go through right now. Give it a couple hours if you're not in a hurry. This didn't happen long ago. Figure he might be coming up this way. We called it in then they told us to do this."

"Got a vehicle type?" Valentine said.

"Nothing so far." Waters said. "Clerk was tied up good when we found him. Didn't see him coming in and couldn't see him leave."

Kasey stood in the background, saying nothing. He was assessing Valentine the way he always did. Not willing to help describe this wild goose chase.

"Like I said," Valentine said, "I'll let you know if I see anything."

Kenny Kasey stepped forward.

Put his hands on the lowered window of Valentine's truck.

"This one I got a weird feeling about, Billy," he said. "Some kinda desperado."

Valentine nodded.

"Anything else, Kenny?"

The older policeman shook his head.

"That's all we know, Billy," Kasey said. "Careful. He's armed and dangerous."

"You know me, Kenny," Valentine said. "Careful's my middle name."

❋ ❋ ❋

At one end of the AM dial, an announcer on the tribal radio station was talking.

From the few English words Valentine recognized, there either would be a tribal council meeting today or there had been one a while ago.

Sometimes there was good rock and roll on this station, but not today. The announcer had been replaced by native drums and a chant.

Valentine twisted the dial to the right until he heard the only other station coming in from Show Low.

Baby Blue sung by George Strait, interrupted by static.

Where the grass is green and the sky is baby blue.

The old man who owned the station loved that song. He played it every day before reading local news and weather.

There would be no radio reception while Valentine threaded his truck through the Salt River Canyon. Only rock walls and hairpin turns. In some spots, barely enough space for two way traffic.

A car had stopped. A Ford with the passenger's side open and a couple standing by the ledge, the man taking a picture of the woman. Valentine drove past. It was crazy how close she was to the edge. Oblivious to the drop behind them. The woman waving toward the man's camera from the edge of the canyon.

A hawk glided in the air behind the couple.

The floor of the canyon thousands of feet below them.

At the base of the canyon, Billy Valentine crossed the iron bridge spanning the Salt River's trickle.

Valentine pulled the truck to the side of the road and put it in park.

A pole and brush wickiup and a derelict white building stood near the brown water. An Esso sign with seven rust-rimmed bullet holes was still nailed to the side of the structure.

Valentine walked down the road until it stopped. Then he saw something. Some kind of vehicle. Not hidden very well, but Valentine figured he wasn't supposed to see it.

He hadn't gone down by Hannigan Meadow after all.

Valentine reached under the glove compartment for the Smith and Wesson. He checked the cylinder and put on the gunbelt and holster.

The tan Jeep had been wedged into the little lean-to next to the Esso sign. You couldn't see the Jeep unless, like Valentine, you had walked around the other side. Even then, it wasn't easy to see with a tarp slung over the back end. The vehicle was in reasonably good shape although it looked like the flat beige had been hand-painted. He walked to the passenger side.

Denim interior with brass grommets just

like regular jeans. In the back seat of the Jeep, fast food wrappers and a dark knit hat. The windows were open but there was nobody nearby.

Valentine shook another cigarette from his pack. Lighted it and leaned back in the seat, looking through the truck window at the canyon walls. He nudged the hat in the back seat. It was a balaclava.

The falcon was now at the top of the canyon, gliding far over Valentine's head.

He looked up at the high walls of the canyon. From where Valentine stood, cars and trucks above him were small.

Valentine stood outside his truck, watched the water, listened. He only heard wind.

He was still maybe a couple hours from Tucson.

* * *

Nicky Fall walked toward the Jeep.

He watched the hawk circling around the Esso sign.

He had to shoot the man.

Nicky didn't know if the man had seen him, but the man had looked at Nicky's Jeep. He'd picked up the balaclava.

Nicky couldn't let the man get away.

All Nicky wanted to do was keep on going.

He looked up at the road which circled above him through the canyon.

The sun was making kaleidoscopic glints in the corners of his eye reaching the top of the sky.

It was past noon.

Nicky didn't need a watch.

He thought about the cars and trucks going in and out of the canyon.

He didn't like the people in the cars. There were too many of them.

The man and the woman running the restaurant had been nosy. Wanting to take his picture.

Nicky couldn't have that.

He had seen this man first in the distance, walking around by the abandoned shack next to the truck. He hoped the man would just turn around and leave.

Maybe the man had just stopped to take a leak, but he'd seen Nicky's Jeep and so now Nicky had to kill him.

Nicky didn't particularly want to kill anybody. He had been glad the big guy behind the counter at the Triangle Market hadn't made a fuss. He was glad the couple at the restaurant hadn't insisted on taking his picture.

Nicky wanted to stay right here tonight. He had stayed in this abandoned shack a few times before. It was pretty comfortable, considering. He had never seen a snake there, for example. People generally stayed away from places like this because of snakes. That was their loss. A snake won't bother you unless you bother it.

He had things to think over.

The job today had been successful.

Taking the money from the guy at the Triangle Market had been easy.

He was still thinking about what the big guy said.

Be my guest.

What kind of thing was that to say when you got a gun pointed at your face?

He might get money from one or two more jobs in a while.

Bigger ones.

Then he would stay out here in the wild longer.

He would only have to go down into civilization for things he really needed.

He hated going where there were a lot of people, and now it would be worse because they would be looking for him.

Nicky heard something.

The man was shouting.

"Put your gun down," the man said. "Put it down and come out slow.

❉ ❉ ❉

Nicky Fall didn't know anything about the man he shot.

He just knew he'd gotten him with one shot, and that was what he wanted to do.

No reason to keep shooting. And no reason

to go look for the man.

Nicky would liked to have taken the man's belt and hat. He'd noticed both of them and they were pretty nice. Money too if the man had it.

But he couldn't wait here. More people would come and then the police would arrive.

Nicky needed to leave right now. He stood up and started to walk toward his Jeep.

Two shots from the Colt had taken the man in the hat down.

At least one of his shots had found it's mark.

The man had to be lying out there somewhere bleeding, but Nicky didn't have time to investigate.

* * *

The highway through the Salt River Canyon winds to the bottom in a series of hairpin turns.

At the bottom of the canyon, cars cross the bridge before winding their way back up to the top of the canyon. Next to the trickle of river, Billy Valentine held his leg. The man's shot had ricocheted, causing a rock shard to pierce his skin.

His flesh was ripped and it hurt like hell, but he would survive.

Valentine was alive and angry.

The man was sitting in the Jeep. Valentine sighted his Smith and Wesson on the man. Steadied the gun. His hands were shaking from the pain.

"Last chance," Valentine said. He didn't shout, but it was loud enough for the man push his gun out the window and take another shot in Valentine's direction.

The man's shot was wild.

Valentine couldn't tell if his returning shots hit the man. Probably they had not.

He lay in the dust, watching the Jeep head up toward the bridge and the canyon road.

Valentine had gotten a look at him. Not a good look, but it was enough.

The man wore a blue t-shirt. Blue, like the sky. Like the George Strait song.

The words on the T-shirt read *Fry Bread Power*.

He wasn't Apache though.

Not this guy.

* * *

Nicky Fall steered the Jeep onto the road and headed up the canyon in the direction of Globe.

He saw the winding road ahead and to the side.

Nicky knew he had been hit, but he didn't know how badly. He looked at his chest which was bleeding through the blue t-shirt. *Fry Bread Power*.

Nicky liked that. If he got out of here he was going to make changes. He was starting to get woozy and it was difficult to keep his mind on the road ahead.

He saw a hawk over the edge of the cliff. The hawk was big and seemed to get bigger in its approach. Nicky blinked his eyes. He wasn't sure if he had ever seen a bird as big as this one. It looked more like some kind of angel, but Nicky didn't believe in angels.

* * *

Tribal Police were the first on the scene. Kasey and Waters stood on a shoulder of the Salt River Canyon looking down at the wreck.

From their position, the men could see all the way down to the bottom of the canyon.

They could see the Jeep and the smoke still curling upward.

Troopers from the State Police would soon arrive and an ambulance, although there was no chance the driver had survived the plunge and subsequent fire.

Waters had been driving when Kenny Kasey got the call.

Waters looked through his binoculars.

They had been pulled off the roadblock and dispatched to the scene after the accident had been reported. The Jeep had gone off the road and tumbled down the canyon. At this point, they couldn't even say in which direction the Jeep had been heading. The road was narrow. A tricky road.

This time of year, the Salt River was a trickle of water meandering through the canyon. From the bottom of the canyon, the walls showed layer upon layer of stratification. Geologic evidence of the river carving the canyon. The canyon would grow deeper even with this trickle.

Time's contribution. You could see the river and the canyon from the top.

Waters adjusted the binoculars then offered them to Kasey.

Kasey put down his cigarette and took the binoculars. Pointed at the Jeep.

"Look at this, Kenny," Waters said. "How fast you think he was going?"

"Fast enough," Massey said.

Kasey pushed the binoculars back toward Waters.

Both policemen stood on the edge of the canyon, black cowboy boots inches from the guard rail. Search and rescue would be able to retrieve what was left of the body, but there would be no way to pull out the Jeep.

January 3, 2022
Fairview, Pennsylvania

A Note to the Reader:

Thanks go to Carolyn Holliday and John Holliday for their assistance in the creation of this book.

Thank you for reading this book.
If you enjoyed *Ten Shots Quick and Other Stories of the New West,* please consider writing a short review on Amazon and telling your friends. As Walter Tevis, writer of *The Hustler* and *The Queen's Gambit* wrote when making the same request: "word of mouth is an author's best friend and is much appreciated."

Trevor Holliday

BOOKS BY THIS AUTHOR

Trinity Works Alone

Trinity Thinks Twice

Trinity And The Short-Timer

Trinity Springs Forward

Trinity And The Heisters

Trinity's Takes Flight

Ferguson's Trip

Dim Lights Thick Smoke

Lefty And The Killers

Printed in Great Britain
by Amazon